24 Hour Te

SAURIA TRADING
COMPANY

D0585855

THE WORLD OF
SUPERSAURS
CLASH OF THE TYRANTS

UNLEASH THE SAURS!

BOOKS:

Raptors of Paradise
The Stegosorcerer
Clash of the Tyrants
Available from all places good books are sold

APP:

Download the free Supersaurs app to experience more
and see the saurs come to life.

Available free on Apple from iTunes App Store and on
Android from Google Play Store.

WEBSITE:

Head to the Supersaurs website for bonus material,
news, events and more!

www.supersaurs.com

THE WORLD OF
SUPERSAURS
CLASH OF THE TYRANTS

JAY JAY BURRIDGE

S

First published in Great Britain in 2018 by
Supersaurs
80-81 Wimpole Street, London, W1G 9RE
www.supersaurs.com

Text and illustrations copyright © Supersaurs Limited, 2018
Illustrations by Chris West & Jay Jay Burridge

A CIP catalogue record for this book is available from the British Library.

ISBN: 978-1-786-96803-6

1 2 3 4 5 6 7 8 9 10
Typeset in Adobe Jenson by Perfect Bound Ltd
Printed and bound by Toppan Leefung

Supersaurs is an imprint of Bonnier Zaffre,
a Bonnier Publishing Company

www.bonnierpublishing.co.uk

*For Mouse, Bear and Fox
and all the other creatures in my life.*

Glitterbone, sparklestone
Twice-birthed child
In a saur's nest you must hide
From there will a Saurman rise

Glitterbone, sparklestone
Twin-starred morn
One life lived but two lives long
Order of the Saurmen born

Glitterbone, sparklestone
Double-yolk egg
By a saur you once were fed
To the Temple you'll be led

Glitterbone, sparklestone
Split-seamed son
A tree you'll find, but only one
When you're called, you must come

Glitterbone, sparklestone
Two-times strong
Know what's right, do no wrong
Pass along this sacred song

~ Wise Woman's Ditty ~
(traditional clapping song, Anon.)

Grace and Franklin

~ Carter, her wonderful baby ~

Koto Lama, Wokan, the Islands of Aru, Maluku
Province of Eastern Indonesia, 1921

Grace Kingsley awoke with a fever, a tangle of wet hair across her face. The hut felt like it was swaying and was filled with the thick, damp air that slowly rose after every monsoon downpour.

There was a thud to the side of the hut's thin palm and timber wall. Grace sat up, blinking the sweat from her eyes. Her baby slept on silently beside her, his chest moving rhythmically. The early-evening sky was turning deep orange, and seeped in through the gaps in the walls.

'Grace, you awake?' asked Jara from the doorway, as she lit a lantern.

'I think so, yes.' Grace slowly folded her legs beneath her on the hard bed and gently stroked Carter's soft cheek. 'Is Franklin back?'

'They're not back yet – you hungry? I have fish stew,' Jara offered.

'Not right now, thanks, Jara. The hut – it was shaking?'

'It was Junti and the other kylos up to no good. Somehow got out of their pen and tried to snuggle under the hut. The saurs are all playing up today. You were asleep when three Rhiptus Rhats flew in – I had to shoo them away from the baby!'

The swaddled infant next to Grace stirred from his deep sleep and his eyes flickered. 'I'll leave you to feed your boy.' Jara smiled kindly and left.

It wasn't long before the orange shards of sunlight faded, and voices could be heard outside. Grace strained to recognise them, but they all were chattering in the local tongue and then one booming voice came closer and broke into English.

'Again! I definitely closed the gate after I got them back in the first time. What were they doing?'

'They were under the hut – probably heard the baby and tried to sneak a peek at it,' Jara joked.

'Don't be silly – that boy hasn't cried once. I doubt the kylos or most of our neighbours know there's been a baby here. Something's spooking the saurs all right. You know, I saw Shadow Raptors in the treeline on my way in to the New Town – they never come this close to the Old Town.'

'I put the Shorthorn Tritops in with the kylos, but you will need to check that the pen's secure,' said Jara. 'Franklin not with you?'

'I told him to stay in town, enjoy the evening, and get a good night's sleep in the guest house. When I left he was in deep conversation with another Westerner, enjoying a celebratory drink with a new friend.'

The hut suddenly jerked forward, sending the hanging lantern's shadows swirling and Billo dashing outside, cursing, into the twilight, 'Stop rubbing up to my hut, you clumsy saur!'

The rest of what he said was in the local dialect.

Grace turned her attention back to Carter, her wonderful baby, who now had his arms free and was lifting them up past his head with a little post-milk satisfied stretch, oblivious to all the rumbling and honking outside. Grace held his tiny hands in hers and patted them together while she entertained him with snatches of an old song.

> *Glitterbone, sparklestone*
> *Twice-birthed child*
> *In a saur's nest you must hide*
> *From there will a Saurman rise*

✦ ✦ ✦

The New Town looked like it was used to visitors of all types, and Franklin could detect numerous languages mixed into a conversation at the back of the bar by a group of men playing cards.

'And where are you from, Lambrecht?' he asked his drinking companion.

'Königsberg, Prussia. And please call me Lambert; it's a lot simpler.'

'And less Germanic?' Franklin said. 'I guess a lot of people want to forget the war. I have a good friend, Theo, who's still fighting it in his head.'

'Yes – that, and I wish I could have chosen my own name. Lambrecht is dull. Now, Carter – that's a great name for a son; definitely got a life of exploration and adventure ahead of him, I say.' Lambert raised his glass. 'To Carter.'

Franklin beamed and lifted his drink to meet Lambert's. 'To Carter.'

'Do you have any children, Lambert?' Franklin asked, after putting his drink down.

Lambert shook his head. 'None.'

'Not interested, or perhaps you've just not found the right woman yet?' Franklin prompted. He was still high on the elation of the last twenty-four hours, and, having held his newborn son for the first time, felt somehow that the usual rules of polite society did not apply. It gave him an uncharacteristic lack of caution when speaking with a stranger.

His companion drew a deep breath. 'No,' he sighed. 'I have a wife with whom I'm very happy. But we have never had children. It suits us this way. My own father was . . . less than perfect, let us say.'

Franklin was intrigued. 'Go on,' he urged, leaning back in his chair.

Lambert paused before elaborating. 'Well, I had five older brothers – one was my twin – but they were all bigger, stronger and more clever than I was, and were my father's favourites. I was sickly, and childhood was not a great time for me. I was often sent away by myself to get the clean alpine air.'

Lambert sipped his drink, lost in the memory.

'My twin brother died when we were seven,' he said. 'It was a terrible accident. My mother died soon after. In his grief, my father blamed me for my mother's death, and I was sent to a boarding school far away in England.'

He stared into his glass. 'When I returned as a young man, I was a complete stranger to everyone in my family.'

Franklin was at a loss for words. He felt he couldn't pry any further into the circumstances of Lambert's tragic childhood. The death of his twin had obviously coloured the man's whole life.

'My father made no attempt to get to know me,' Lambert continued, shifting in his seat, 'and left me to make my own way in the world while he concentrated on making sure my brothers had high positions in the family business. They went to war, but I missed the conscription. When they returned home triumphant, my father drew them all close – but not me.'

Lambert looked up with a weak smile while Franklin listened intently.

'Unfortunately for him, my father then watched everyone close to him die, one by one. My brothers all met untimely ends. The worst bad luck befell them. Eventually my father *had* to notice me, as I was the very last one left. He was a bitter man. He told everyone I was useless and would amount to nothing, despite my having my own measure of success. He held on to the family business even as he grew old and frail, until one day my fortune changed.'

Lambert sat upright and pulled a cigarette case from his jacket pocket, tipping it to Franklin, who declined.

'My father's house burned down with him in it,' Lambert said, as he touched the blue flame that sparked from his lighter to his cigarette.

'I inherited everything,' he said softly, as he exhaled a curl of smoke. 'Being the sixth son I was never supposed to inherit my father's title – Viscount – but the weakest somehow survived them all.'

Lambert swirled the remaining beer in his glass as his eyes followed the wisp of smoke as it lifted up and away into the rafters.

'How terrible,' Franklin murmured, not knowing what

else to say. It certainly was an astonishing tale. It made him appreciate his own upbringing, with loving parents who had supported his dreams. How he looked forward to presenting Bunty and Sidney with their new grandson! His heart ached at the thought of little Bea, whom he missed terribly, although he knew she was in safe hands.

Lambert looked at him and smiled. 'Yes, very sad for them,' he said with a wink, 'but not so bad for me. Come, Franklin, let's drink to birth and death.' They both clinked their glasses.

'Birth and death.'

'Surely you must have missed your twin?' Franklin said, now that the tension had lifted.

'Can't say I miss any of my family,' Lambert declared stoically.

'My brother has two twin girls,' Franklin offered. 'Identical. I also have a two-year-old daughter, Beatrice, back in England.'

'Stick with two children.' Lambert winked. 'You can keep an eye on each one.'

Franklin, feeling the need to reciprocate such a personal story with a revelation of his own, and prompted by the talk of twins, undid a shirt button and lifted a well-worn leather cord from round his neck.

'Here, look at this,' he said.

Hanging from the cord was a strange dark stone that glinted and dazzled sharply in the dim light. He set it down on the bar in front of Lambert, who stared into its entrancing surface.

'I found this pendant in America. It's one of a pair. They both had these strange matching stones – look, it's actually a small bone!'

Lambert gently lifted the pendant into the light, which seemed to burn deep into it and then illuminate it from within. There was blackness and brilliance of pinks and purples mixed with pinheads of jade and turquoise. 'My goodness, it does sparkle,' he said admiringly.

'That it does,' Franklin continued. 'The other pendant has the other half of this bone: they join up together to make one. They are two halves of the same thing – one and two, you understand?'

Franklin nodded to the barman to pour them both another drink, while Lambert was hypnotised by the stone's allure. Abruptly he tore his attention away from it.

'Sorry, I don't quite follow. Why do you have only one of the pendants? Surely they belong together?'

'I can't explain why I took only one,' Franklin explained. 'Something drew me to it; I *had* to have it.'

Lambert looked on with a puzzled expression. 'So you stole it?'

Franklin laughed. 'You could call it that, I suppose. But it was clear the previous owners had no use for them any more. The twins were long dead. I told you,' Franklin explained, 'I'm an explorer, a treasure hunter. Even the great Howard Carter –' At the name of his hero, he raised his glass into the air to toast him.

Lambert raised his glass to join it. 'To Carter!'

They both knocked back their drinks and slammed down the glasses.

'Even the man who discovered the tomb of the great pharaoh Tutankhamun gets called a grave robber,' Franklin continued. 'I'm just trying to discover the mystery surrounding this bone and the secrets it unlocks.'

Lambert looked more intently at the strange object. 'It is rather magical. What's it made from – stone or bone?'

'You see, it's even got you entranced! This, my new friend, is no ordinary stone and no ordinary bone; it's both.'

'How can that be?' Lambert asked, as Franklin took it from his hand and held it up so that the last of the day's fading light could grace its surface and release a dazzling bloom of sparkles.

'It's a semi-precious stone called an opal,' Franklin explained. 'Recently they found some more like this in the lightning fields of Australia. I've been to check them out.'

'So it's a stone,' Lambert confirmed.

Franklin nodded. 'Yes, but not just that; it's also a fossilised and opalised dinosaur bone.'

Lambert frowned at him, puzzled. 'How does a bone become an opal?'

'That's exactly what I wanted to find out,' Franklin gushed, excited to have the opportunity to talk about

his obsession. 'And more to the point – why were these extremely rare opalised bones traded around the world? And why did this particular one – well, half of one – end up in America, hundreds, and possibly thousands, of years ago?'

'I have a feeling you're going to tell me. We're going to need another drink,' Lambert said, and signalled to the barman, who refilled their glasses as Franklin talked.

'It turns out this object is known as a Saurman's keystone. Some ancient texts refer to it as a key bone,' he said. 'Stone or bone, it's no different.'

'Am I supposed to know what a key bone or keystone is?' Lambert asked.

'No – and, in fact, there are probably only a few people in the world who know that it should belong to a Saurman.' Franklin lowered his head and whispered, 'It's all a well-kept secret.' He winked and went to tap his nose, but missed twice. The local spirits were having an effect.

'Go on.' Lambert was intrigued.

'There's not a lot left of the Saurman Empire,' said Franklin. 'It stretched wherever civilisation was around the world, but disappeared thousands of years ago. It was soaked up over the years by other cultures and religions and diluted into myth. But some fragments of the Saurman Empire remain, kept alive by the Secret Order of Saurmen.'

'Amazing,' Lambert muttered in a hushed voice, 'and this keystone does what exactly?'

Franklin's eyes lit up. He was on a roll and couldn't help himself from going on.

'It has a strange power. I think what each one can do depends on the owner, because all the accounts differ. The one constant is that the Saurmen, who used to wear them, apparently lived for a very, very long time. One day I'm going to pass this keystone on to my son, Carter.'

Lambert took a drag on his cigarette. 'That is very interesting,' he said, before exhaling slowly.

2

A Stinky Fish

~ why the half-eaten post is always late ~

Brownlee Estate, Oxfordshire, England, 1933

Birds sang safely overhead in the trees as the postman looked cautiously through the iron bars of the large gate. He looked at his wrist watch. It was 5.50 a.m., far earlier than he usually began work, but today he had to

deliver a bundle of mail that had been gathering for some time at the Post Office. The arrival of a letter marked 'URGENT' had prompted the postmaster to demand that it all had to be delivered today, no matter what, and this postman had drawn the short straw. He'd been here before, and was not keen to relive the experience. This time, he was not only very early, but better prepared and equipped for the task.

The coast looked clear, so he gently leant his bike against a stone pillar and lowered his bag to the floor. From the front pocket he pulled an oil dispenser and gently squeezed the handle so that an ample amount of the thick black lubricant spilled over the gate's hinges. He also remembered the squeaky latch and gave it an extra-thick dose. Today the gate was not going to make a sound. He gave his own bike's moving parts a second coat of oil, then opened up the main pouch of his canvas bag. Instead of the post, he pulled out his cricket leg pads and tied them up with double knots. He squatted to make sure he could still bend his legs, and then brought out a thick overcoat and leather rugby head guard from the bag. Finally he put on his padded cricket gloves and patted himself down. He had doubled in size. It was a little more difficult getting his bag back over his shoulders, so he had to remove the gloves. With a final double check that everything on the gate was glistening with oil, he took a deep breath, raised the latch silently, and swung it open.

Once safely through, he mounted his bike and gently pushed off up the path that swung round the side of the lake and along an avenue of stately oaks towards the large house. The morning light caught the sides of the trees and sparkled off the surface of the lake. A lonesome duck quacked and raised its cramped wings for a stretch and flap. The movement caught the postman's eye, and he nervously looked over his shoulder as the duck settled back on the glass-like water and quacked again. Happy that he had not been noticed he pedalled calmly and silently up the path.

Suddenly the duck was pulled under the water with great force.

Buster's eyes rolled back as he licked his lips and raised himself out of the water. With a few strides, he made his way to the edge of the lake and shook the water from his heavy coat of black feathers in a rainbow arc of water droplets and moved over to a sunny spot to dry off. That's when the tyrant noticed the postman.

✦ ✦ ✦

The doorbell rang and was followed by loud banging on the door.

'Coming!' Theodore shouted. He slid the chain and went to turn the key, but it rattled out of the lock and dropped to the floor. 'Stop banging – nothing's *this* urgent!' he yelled over the thumping noise as he placed the key back in the lock and turned it. With that the door burst open to the utter relief of the postman, who had been pinned up against it, being licked up and down by the mighty tyrant.

'You're early,' Theodore noted, as the postman fell through the doorway and scrambled across the floor to the back of the hall, panting. Buster leant his head in and let out what those who loved him would describe as a playful sound, but what to everyone else sounded like a horrifying

blood-curdling roar. The postman scrabbled back even
further, shaking in fear.

'That's a good boy, Buster.' Theodore patted the tyrant
on the nose.

Buster opened his mouth extra wide and regurgitated
half of the postman's sack. He retched a second time, and
some letters and duck feathers came up and landed in a
pool of saliva on the doorstep.

'Thank you for that, Buster,' Theodore muttered,
lifting his foot to swipe the post and bag into the doorway.

The postman was trembling and trying his best to get to his feet, but was held down by a half-chewed cricket leg pad that was twisted and torn around him.

'Let me help you.' Theodore lifted the man. 'He likes fish, the smellier the better,' he advised.

'What?'

'Fish. He's eaten all the trout in the lake. I'm sure if you came with a stinky fish and tossed it to him, he would leave you alone and probably love you for ever.' Theodore smiled. 'I'm presuming you're the postman. Your uniform is somewhat unconventional.'

'Yes, I am your postman,' the man confirmed, as he untangled and removed the torn pad and stood tall.

'Don't see you that much,' Theodore said, dabbing his toe at the pool of drool in which some letters lay.

'No, on account of that tyrant you keep,' the postman said. 'We draw straws to see who has to come once a fortnight.'

'Ahh . . . so that explains why the half-eaten post is always late.' Theodore smiled. 'Don't mind Buster. The kitchen is through there and there's tea in the pot. Get yourself straight and I'll get Carter to take Buster back to the stable.'

Bea came downstairs, adjusting her school uniform and carrying a tray on which was a selection of burnt bread.

'Special toast again?' she called out sarcastically.

'If you're not happy with my special toast, then there's

a larder with plenty of other food in it, but don't ask me to burn it for you,' Theodore grunted. 'Have you seen Carter?'

'No. Who was that at the door?'

'What was left of the postman.'

'Good, has my comic arrived?'

'Half of it. You'll have to ask Buster for the rest. He's outside. Can you take him to the stable? The postman needs to get back to work.'

Bea scowled. It had been hard adjusting to life without Bunty, and having Theodore in charge, especially as they didn't always see eye to eye about things. Suddenly having to assume the role of parent was hard for him too, she supposed, but she knew he tried his best and did what he thought was right. Even if Bea didn't always agree with him.

Theodore wiped down what was left of the mail that Buster had delivered in his own unique way onto the doorstep. There were four letters, two of which had American stamps on them – one of these was in a fancy silver envelope, and the other, a pale blue one, was half eaten. Theodore had a good idea who they were from, so his attention turned to the remains of a brown envelope that was well beyond saving, and finally the one that was marked URGENT in big letters. Theodore opened this first, his eyes glancing over the headed paper, and his heart sank instantly. Reading the contents of the letter didn't help lift his spirits. He stuffed it into his back pocket and turned to the two American letters. Perhaps these would bring better news – but just in case he'd better have that cup of tea he had been brewing before the day went sideways.

In the kitchen, the postman had stopped shaking and was finishing his tea. He had removed his torn outer clothes and was looking more like a conventional postman.

'Thanks for the brew, and the advice,' he said. 'The stinkier the better, right?'

'Right,' Theodore replied. 'The tyrant's being led back to the stable, so you can go safely now.'

The man nodded and left. Theodore poured a cup of tea for himself from the pot and looked at the back of the blue envelope. The return address read 'Kingsley Ranch', a place to which Theodore longed to turn back time and go.

Bea strolled in with Carter, who was in part of his school uniform – only now his trousers were homemade shorts and a tie had replaced his belt. There was straw in his hair.

'He slept in the stables again,' said Bea, as she went to pour herself a cup of tea. She noticed the blue envelope in Theodore's hand.

'A letter from Uncle Cash!' she cried in delight. 'Is he asking for us to visit again?'

'How do I know? It's not opened yet,' Theodore retorted. 'Besides –'

'Besides what?'

Bea crossed her arms to make it clear that Theodore

had better be prepared for how upset she was about to become.

'Besides,' Theodore went on, removing the other letter from his back pocket, 'I have something else on my mind.' He held it out so that Bea could see the school's crest.

Bea's expression changed.

'I see you're both dressed for school.' Theodore spoke in a measured tone. 'Yet this letter informs me you no longer go to school. In fact, you were expelled last week. So where exactly have you been going every morning?'

Bea uncrossed her arms. 'I've been taking Carter out and about,' she replied. 'He learns more outside school with me teaching him.'

'Great, and who teaches *you*, Beatrice?' Theodore replied, frowning. 'The headteacher says there was a fight. When were you going to tell me?'

'They started it,' Bea cried sullenly. 'Senior boys were picking on Carter.'

'You should have told a teacher, not started a fight.' Theodore sighed. 'Bea, you had top grades; you were an A student – now you're expelled! Besides, Carter can fend for himself.'

A heavy silence lingered as Theodore and Bea each tried to figure out what to do next. Carter was silent, watching.

'We could go to visit Uncle Cash,' Bea said, shrugging her shoulders with eyebrows raised, 'have some fun, go on an adventure?'

For the first time in ages, Theodore heard the old Bea, the one who had something sensible and honest to say, not the new one who was always angry with him. He sighed, knowing the new Bea was about to bounce straight back when he replied.

'Absolutely not, young lady – you are staying right here and sorting your problems out,' he said sternly.

'My problems?' she cried. 'What about *your* problems? Since we came back from Africa there's been nothing *but* problems in this house! Let's go to America and leave all the problems behind!'

Carter looked between them and quietly spoke. 'No school?'

'No more adventures,' Theodore spat. 'We're definitely *not* going to America!'

And with that Theodore slammed the pale blue unopened letter onto the table, rattling the cups of tea like a peal of ceramic bells sounding an alarm.

3

The Wonderful
Wild West

~ just like old times ~

California, North America, 1933

Bea looked out of the window at the craggy landscape and smiled. 'It's been four years since I was last at Uncle Cash and Aunt Bonnie's. So much has happened since then – I can't wait to tell my cousins.'

'Not long now,' said Theodore.

It had taken some convincing, but Bea had managed to persuade Theodore that family came first. And since Carter considered Buster to be family, he'd had to come along too. Besides, there was no way that Carter was going to allow someone else to take care of his tyrant for months at a time.

Suddenly the train started to brake hard with a long sharp squeal of metal on metal, jolting everyone forward with such violence that the passengers tumbled out of their seats and fell to the floor. The luggage stored on the overhead racks rained down, crashing around them.

Luckily Bea and Carter had the quickness of mind to dive under the table for protection. Eventually the train slowed down to a safe halt and the screeching stopped.

Theodore pushed himself to his feet and stood surveying the mayhem in the carriage, checking for anyone who might be seriously hurt. He noticed that everyone seemed to be stumbling back to their feet, even though many seemed quite shaky.

The interconnecting door burst open and the train conductor appeared.

'Everyone all right?' he called anxiously.

'Seems to be,' said Theodore. 'What happened? Did we hit something on the track?'

'Almost,' said the conductor. 'We went round the bend and there was a carriage on its own right in front of us, on fire!'

'On fire! We'd better go and check on Buster – he won't know what's going on and is liable to be spooked.'

Theodore, Bea and Carter headed for the livestock carriage and soon saw the burning cargo carriage on the tracks ahead. Its metal frame was intact but the smashed wooden roof and panels burned wildly.

'You go on,' Theodore told Bea and Carter. 'I'll see if there's anything I can do to help.'

Theodore stepped down from the train but the engine driver and fireman stopped him as he made for the burning wreckage.

'Sorry, sir,' said the driver. 'I wouldn't get any closer than that.'

'Whose is it?' asked Theodore.

The train driver shrugged.

'Where are we, exactly?' Theodore asked.

'About thirty miles short of Jackson.'

'How long will we be here?'

The driver shook his head. 'From the look of it, this train's not going anywhere for a while,' he said. 'Lucky no one was hurt, at least.'

Theodore headed to the livestock carriage and told Bea and Carter the news. 'So we could be here quite some time,' he finished.

'Let's ride Buster,' suggested Carter energetically. 'If we're going to be stuck here we could take him out for a bit.'

Theodore went to say *no*, but then saw an old buckboard cart at the back of the carriage and had an idea. It wasn't in a great state but it might just get them and their luggage to the ranch.

Soon after, the train was a shimmering reflection on the horizon and they were immersed in the wonderful Wild West.

Theodore grinned from ear to ear. 'It's just like old times, riding with a saur across the open range,' he chuckled. 'Oh, how I've missed the place!'

✦ ✦ ✦

Bea spotted the Kingsley ranch first. It was just as she remembered: a large double-storey house made of slatted wood, painted white, the roof covered with red wooden shingles and surrounded by a picket fence. Around this were paddocks with a variety of different tritops in them. The small lake was almost empty and four hadros wallowed in the remaining mud as a flock of birds settled and picked at the insects hovering above the ground.

'Oh my goodness, that's a sight you don't see any more!' she squealed. 'Apatos, look at the size of them!'

Theodore pointed to the heads rising above the roof of a series of large barns. As they turned round and joined the main path the scale of the apatosaurs became apparent. Carter looked back to Bea and Theodore with a huge smile on his face. The excitement was too much and he egged Buster to go faster, and then into a gallop, holding on to his thick coat of jet-black feathers. He careened to a

stop at his Uncle Cash's feet, the buckboard cart skidding wildly to the side in the dust as one wheel snapped off its axle and pirouetted into a fence.

'Now that's what I call an entrance!' Uncle Cash bellowed as Theodore dusted himself down and Bea ran over to hug him.

'Why don't you head round the back and surprise your cousins while I meet your brother?' Cash suggested, striding over to Carter, who was disentangling himself from Buster's reins.

'So you're my nephew Carter, I assume?' Cash knelt down, looked deep into Carter's blue eyes, and took in a deep breath. 'You know who I am?'

Carter shook his head.

'I'm the closest thing you have left of your father,' he said. 'It's mighty fine to meet you after all these years.' With that he embraced the boy tightly. 'That's eleven years of hugs right there, boy!'

Carter grinned.

'Why don't you put your friend in the pen round back before he trips over anything else?'

Carter clicked his fingers, and Buster scampered over to join him. He vaulted onto Buster's back, and then headed off round the back of the house towards the pen.

Cash Kingsley shook his head in stunned admiration.

Theodore strolled over and embraced his old friend.

'Well, I ain't never seen that before,' Cash said to him, 'a boy and a tyrant so close as that.'

'It's very rare,' agreed Theodore. 'There's definitely something special about Carter.'

'You still telling folks he was found wandering wild in Australia?' asked Cash.

'Yes. Mainly because no one would believe the true story,' Theodore replied.

Cash smiled. 'Looks like that boy's gonna fit in just fine. He's with his family now.'

Bea was busy shrieking with excitement alongside her identical twin cousins, Violet and May, who were about a year older than her.

'Violet and May, I present your other cousin, Carter.' Bea got up and proudly nudged her brother closer to them.

Carter wiped the dust-soaked sweat from his face and nervously patted himself down before offering his hand to shake. The girls both giggled as they stood up and said, 'Pleasure to meet you, Carter,' in unison.

Carter stared at them both, looking back and forth with his mouth open while trying to find the right words. 'Who is who?' he managed to say.

All the girls laughed. Bea realised Carter had never seen identical twins before and that this would take another level of explanation.

'I think you're going to have to wear different colour clothes for the next few days,' Bea told them, and grinned.

Aunt Bonnie came through the screen door and smiled. 'My heavens, Bea, you've grown!' she exclaimed. 'You were just a little girl, but – my word – you're almost a young lady!' Bea went in for the hug she had been dreaming of. 'And, Carter, come here!' Bonnie beckoned him over. 'Come, come, let me see you.' She took him in her arms.

Carter was beginning to get the hang of this. For Bea, it had been too long since she had felt truly at home, and seeing how easily Carter smiled she imagined how much her beloved grandmother Bunty would have enjoyed seeing them all together, and her spirits lifted.

A little while later, Bonnie rang the dinner bell.

Set on a long table in the shade of a large tree was a feast for the hungry travellers.

'My word, that's a good sight,' Theodore said as he sat down. Meanwhile, Cash took out his Bowie knife and cut the chickens into big juicy pieces.

'You look like a leg man to me, Carter,' said Cash as he popped one onto the plate that Bea had already piled up for him with potato salad and sweetcorn.

As Carter picked up the chicken leg and began to chew, May and Violet gazed at him with looks of awe.

'Were you really brought up in the jungle?' asked May.

'By raptors?' asked Violet.

'Uh-huh,' Carter said, nodding, his mouth too full to

be able to speak properly.

'Slow down, Carter,' Theodore admonished.

'Never mind him,' Bonnie reassured the boy. 'If you're hungry, eat!' She shot Theodore a fond but exasperated look.

'No other humans?' asked May.

'No,' said Carter, after he'd swallowed the food in his mouth. 'There were other people on the island, but we stayed away from them because we thought they were dangerous.'

'We?'

'Me and the raptors who raised me. So I never had anything to do with humans until Bea and Theodore and Bunty turned up.'

'Wow!' said Violet. She beamed happily. 'Everyone around here is gonna be so jealous of us! We got a raptor for a cousin!'

'Cash, it's so good to see you and the family again,' Theodore said, patting Cash on the back after they'd eaten. 'Everything seems a lot bigger. I like the two new barns over there, and, if I'm not mistaken, you have apatos in the paddock. I though those giants were almost extinct.'

'Thanks,' Cash said, stretching his legs. 'We've had some success trying to rear apatos but they don't half take up space! We're having some trouble so I'm keeping them close by and in the barns overnight for now.'

'What sort of trouble?'

'Drought. Everyone around here's been affected,'

Cash explained. 'We've had a few dry years and the water table has got pretty low. The rains have returned, but the streams still ain't what they used to be. Plus something has been attacking the livestock.'

Theodore looked at Cash with a puzzled expression. 'What kind of something?'

'Tell you what, Theo, let's not discuss this here. I have to head into Jackson later. There are some goods I need to pick up. Let's both go in and I'll bring you up to date with what's been going on around here. We could catch a drink in the bar for old time's sake while we're at it.'

Theodore smiled. 'Just like the good old days,' he said, but then frowned. 'But sadly without Franklin or Grace.' He looked across the table, hearing the children's laughter, and frowned.

Cash nodded pensively. 'And you can tell me what's troubling you, Theo,' he added. 'You look like you need that drink more than I do.'

4

Peabody's Curse

~ the bar on Main Street ~

After the long lunch, Cash fixed up the old buckboard cart, hitched it to one of the hadrosaurs, and waved at Theodore, who was sitting in the shade of a big tree listening to the children energetically recounting parts of their adventures in Aru and Kenya to Bonnie and the twins.

'Boy, oh boy, Cash, your girls are so grown up now,' Theodore said, climbing up beside him on the cart.

'I'm glad you decided to come,' said Cash, as they moved off. 'And in time for the county fair.'

'That's still going?'

'It's been quiet the past few years – the Depression's meant not a lot of people around these parts had the money or reason to celebrate. But we're coming out of it, and this year promises to be like old times – local produce, livestock, carnival rides and, of course, the rodeo. I remember you used to be good at riding the bull tritops.'

'Not as good as Franklin,' said Theodore. 'He was the master.'

Cash gave a long sigh. 'All those years of mystery, and now we finally know what happened. Attacked and killed in the jungle in Aru.'

Theodore shook his head. 'I don't know that for sure, Cash. Something inside me is telling me that the truth is still out there and . . . and –'

'And what?' Cash cut in.

'And we owe it to them to find out everything.'

Cash was silent for a while in contemplation. 'So, this Viscount friend of yours, Carter's godfather – are you saying he was wrong about what happened? He's been in contact with me a lot, wants to talk business even.'

'He has?' Theodore rolled his eyes. 'He'd asked for your address. He's been sending gifts to Bea and Carter – too many.'

'Well, I'm not surprised, he's got a lot of making up to do,' said Cash angrily. 'That's a man with a guilty conscience, running away and leaving a baby in the jungle to a pack of wild raptors.'

'He was wounded; he couldn't have fought them all off,' Theodore reasoned. 'He was lucky to get out alive himself by the sounds of it.'

'Okay, but he didn't even bother to find Franklin's or Grace's relatives, tell them . . . tell *us* what happened. He sounds as if he's got enough money – he could have hired someone to track us down. Hell, he owes us the last eleven years of worry!' Cash was getting worked up.

'Agreed. I would have tried to find the next of kin and inform them but –' Theodore tried to find words to defend Lambert in his absence. 'He was with us at the lodge when it burned, when we lost Bunty. He saved my life, pulling me from the fire. Without him, those children would have lost everyone.'

'That may be so, Theo, but he ain't saved *my* life, so if you don't mind I'm going to give him a piece of my mind when he arrives.'

Theodore jumped in his seat. 'Arrives here? When?'

'Don't look so surprised – I wrote, remember?'

Theodore shook his head and sighed.

'We have a problem with our mail. Buster usually eats it; we were lucky to get half your letters.'

'Look,' Cash said, 'I didn't want this Viscount to come, but Bonnie insisted we be hospitable, so there it is.'

As they rode on they caught up on the news. There had been the odd letter and telegrams between them, but usually Bunty had kept everyone informed of everyone's business, and without her it had been a hard adjustment for both men, even without Buster's appetite for post.

The state sheriff's vehicle was parked up on the side of the road and there was something a few hundred yards from the road that had garnered their attention. As they got closer it became apparent something was wrong, so Cash turned the cart off the road and dismounted to see if they could be of assistance. The sheriff was returning to his vehicle and wafting his hat in front of his face.

'Afternoon, Cash,' called the sheriff. 'Thought I would come and inspect this one myself, it being so close to Jackson.' He wiped the sweat away from his forehead before popping his hat back on again. 'It's real nasty.'

Cash turned to Theodore. 'You were asking earlier – now you get to make up your own mind.'

They walked on just past a rocky outcrop and came upon the most ghastly sight.

Blood, baked in the heat of the day, covered everything. There were tritops parts strewn all about – a leg here, a head there. Their bodies were torn apart, with gaping open wounds and deep slash marks where something had mutilated them. By the looks of things, they had been there for at least a day or so.

They were both silent out of respect for the slain saurs, until Theodore spoke. 'Could a pack of wolves take down a tritops like this?'

Cash shook his head.

'Bears? I know a desperate and hungry grizzly bear can do a lot of damage,' Theodore continued.

'If I didn't know better, Theo, I would say that a Lythronax did this,' Cash ventured. 'Mountain Tyrant.'

Theodore cut in quickly. 'Just one? There are three tritops here, I think. A tyrant can only take down one tritops at a time. Why didn't the other two run away? There must have been more than one tyrant to inflict this much damage.'

'Exactly,' Cash confirmed. 'But there've been no wild tyrants here for at least fifty years. Brown Tyrants are solitary; they don't hunt in packs. Mountain Tyrants do but we're well away from the mountains.'

Theodore thought for a moment. 'Didn't there used to be some in the Washoe reserve further north – could they come this far south unnoticed?'

Cash shook his head and looked to the ground. 'Unlikely. We would be seeing them in the day scavenging carrion, and we'd at least find their tracks.'

The two men walked round again in a wider circle, scanning the ground, but found nothing unusual, so they made their way back to the buckboard cart and headed into town. There was just one question on both of their minds: what kind of creature had torn the tritops to pieces and then just disappeared without trace?

✦ ✦ ✦

The bar on Main Street was just the same as ever.

'Afternoon,' the barman said, staring at Theodore and rubbing his chin. 'Hang on, I know you,' he added, but before he could think any further, someone from the back of the bar called out.

'If it ain't the Cockney Cowboy himself, Theo Logan, I'll be damned!'

The man strode over, wearing a wide-brimmed Stetson and an equally large smile. He looked like a classic cowboy from the past.

Theodore smiled back.

'Cody – good to see you! Drink?'

'Don't mind if I do,' Cody beamed. 'Well, well, well, where've you been?'

'Had to go back home, do my bit in the war.'

'A real hero, eh? But the war's been over a long time, Logan – where else?'

'Well, recovering from the war and travelling around the world looking for Franklin and Grace,' he replied affably.

'I sure was sorry to hear from Cash about what happened to them in that jungle,' Cody said. He paused for a moment seeing Cash come over.

'And I was sorry to hear that Bunty passed away too. She was one heck of a lady. She and Sidney raised some mighty fine allos in their day. Say, Cash – you hear about the latest attack?'

'Passed it on the way in. Sheriff was out there taking a look,' said Cash.

'Fat lot of good that's going to do. He's too spooked to

do anything; keeps telling everyone it's Peabody's Curse and that's really bad for business.' Cody sank back his drink in one gulp and gestured to the barman to refill it.

'What's Peabody's Curse?' Theodore asked.

'When some of Old Man Peabody's land came up for sale a good few years back, this rich guy snapped it up and built a shiny new slaughterhouse on it,' Cody explained. 'It was damn good for business, and it meant the tritops didn't have to make that treacherous journey tightly packed up into trains. Broke my heart to see them end their days like that. The trains were fitted out to transport frozen carcasses across the country. Anyhow, the water that brought gold and prosperity to the land now runs red, as the curse said it would.'

'Cody, get to the point,' said Cash, rolling his eyes.

'Sorry. Well, way, way back, the water ran crystal clear and Peabody – the first prospector to come here – found a big nugget of gold in the stream.' Cody held up his clenched fist. 'Big as that, so the story goes. Anyhow, that started the gold rush, which brought hundreds of folks up here to try their luck in the hills. But no one got as lucky as Peabody, and they all lost their investment. So an angry mob killed Peabody and dumped him in the river. It ran red with his blood. Ever since then people been saying when the river runs red again, Old Man Peabody will be back.'

'Back to do what?' Theodore questioned.

'I don't know – revenge or something,' said Cody.

'So why is the water red now?' Theodore asked.

'Well, the slaughterhouse closed a month back,' Cody said. 'It needed water just like the rest of us and its reserves all dried up. There is literally nothing to wash away the blood. Now with the mutilations spilling more blood, we can't even sell our cattle and tritops.' He paused, then went on. 'Last time I went to the market in Sacramento people were saying it was Peabody's Curse, all pointing fingers, none of them buying out of fear.'

5

The Kingsley Twin Riders

~ Bonnie's daily fear ~

The next day started early, even though they all went to bed late telling stories and catching up. The twins had practice and nothing was going to stop that.

'What's so important?' Theodore asked Bonnie as he poured a cup of coffee.

'Don't let the Kingsley Twin Riders hear you say that. Trick-riding is all they care about,' she replied. 'They're practising non-stop for the county fair.'

Theodore took his coffee outside and watched from the porch as Carter and Bea came out of the stables with May and Violet, who were both on almost identical allosaurs. The circular path round the water tank was just wide enough for them to ride the allosaurs at quite a pace. As they spun round they slowly pulled their left legs up and over the saddle to join their right legs. It was quite a sight to see them matching each other's movements and then hopping up onto their saddles.

Bea gasped and Carter clapped loudly. Theodore

raised an eyebrow as Bonnie joined him on the porch. 'That's some nifty riding,' he said, impressed.

The twins reached out to the allos' heads, before sliding down their long necks so that they were holding on to the base of the allos' shoulder blades and did what looked impossible: they swung round to the front of the saurs and hung under their necks, perfectly in time with each other.

Bea turned to Carter in amazement, but he had gone. She looked around, but wherever he had gone was not as important as the spectacle before her.

The twins' performance was only just starting. They managed to get both allosaurs to run together side by side and then hop between them both, one at a time and then together.

'This bit is tricky,' Violet called out to Bea.

'We have to take it slow,' said May.

The allosaurs parted slightly and the girls, who were holding hands, parted with them, but kept holding hands. As they drew further apart they slipped down to the side of the allos, forming a bridge between them.

'This is the bit I can't watch,' Bonnie said, and took Theodore's now empty coffee cup to refill.

Bea held her hands over her mouth in awe as the twins were now only holding on to the saurs with their feet and to each other by their hands. If the allos moved further apart, they would split; if they moved closer together, they would close in and hit the floor. It was practice and precision to the finest degree. After three full laps the girls swung themselves round enough to dismount and land sure-footed on the ground in a perfect pose.

Theodore clapped as loud as he could. 'Amazing, absolutely fantastic!' he cheered.

Bea ran over to them, shouting. 'That was the best thing I have ever seen!'

'Thanks,' the twins said together. 'Wanna try?'

Bea froze. 'There is no way I could do that!'

'Sure you can,' Carter called out from behind them.

He was sitting bareback on Buster. 'Buster also wants to.'

Bonnie returned with coffee. 'Thank goodness that's over. It would be better if they ran away to the circus so I wouldn't have to watch the endless near-death accidents. No mother should see girls fall over and seriously hurt themselves day in, day out.'

'They looked pretty good to me,' Theodore replied, and nodded appreciation for the second cup. 'Good coffee.'

'Those girls are as hard as nails, and it looks like Bea is as well,' she said, pointing to the water tank.

Theodore almost spat out his coffee. Bea had joined in, sitting atop Buster, with Carter clapping loudly along.

♦ ♦ ♦

After several mornings of practice with the new line-up, the Kingsley *Cousin* Riders, Theodore fully understood Bonnie's daily fear. They upped the danger every time, practising their new routine over and over, determined to be the best trick-riders at the county fair.

Bunty's will had left Theodore in charge of Beatrice – of course, Bunty hadn't known of Carter's existence when it was drawn up. It was a role Theodore had not been prepared for. Having to be responsible for the lives of not one but two children was a challenge – especially at times like this, when they seemed hell-bent on danger. He could barely watch.

Theodore turned away for a moment to try to see if he could relax, and that's when she fell.

'I'm all right!' Bea shouted, as Theodore ran over.

'No, you're not – you've cut your knee, look!' he shouted.

She gritted her teeth at him. 'I'm *fine*.'

'It's not safe –' he held out a finger – 'not one little bit. I absolutely forbid you to do it any more! You're not to perform tomorrow.'

'You can't forbid me to do anything; you're not my father!' Bea cried, more hurt by being brought up in front of her cousins than any injury she might have.

'And as for you, Carter,' Theodore said, turning on the boy, 'I'd never have allowed you to bring Buster if I'd known you were going to encourage him like this.'

Carter shrank at this admonishment, clutching at Buster's side.

Bonnie rushed over with a wet cloth, and gave Theodore an exasperated look. 'Now, come here, Bea,' she said lovingly. 'Let's fix you up.'

◆ ◆ ◆

When the dust had settled, Theodore found Carter sitting in a tree looking at the apatos in wonder. He regretted scaring the boy, especially for something that wasn't really his fault.

Just then Carter pointed to a shining object spitting up a dust cloud behind it in the distance. 'What's that?'

'It's a car of sorts,' Theodore replied, squinting.

'Whose car?' Carter asked.

Cash saw what they were looking at and ambled over

to gaze at the sight coming towards them. 'That looks like a Pickwick Nite Coach,' he said incredulously. 'It's a double-decker luxury house on wheels sort of thing.'

'Looks like you've got visitors,' said Theodore.

'I don't know anyone with a Pickwick,' said Cash. 'Or anyone rich enough to own one.'

'Yes, you do,' said Theodore. 'You'd better be on your best behaviour and get out the red carpet, because here comes the Viscount Lamprecht Knútr, or Lambert to his friends.'

'Then I'll call him Lampshade or whatever his name is,' Cash said through gritted teeth.

6

The Knútrs

~ the Pickwick Nite Coach ~

Within no time, the Pickwick was beside them, and from a lower-deck window Lambert leant out and waved. The children were as excited as if it had been Santa Claus himself on a sleigh. Bea had prepped her cousins with stories of the lavish gifts that had kept arriving when they returned from Africa.

They were not disappointed.

When the driver pulled up in front of the ranch and opened the side door, out stepped the most pale, pristine woman they had ever seen, dressed all in black. She stood taller than the driver and waited for Lambert to follow before offering an expression of any kind. As the Viscount popped his head out of the door he saw all the faces staring at him. 'Children, how lovely to see you!' he called out as they ran over. 'This is my wife, Anya Stitz.' And with that she smiled briefly.

Cash was on his best behaviour and it really showed. Even May and Violet could tell their father was overdoing it somewhat. Saying 'May I help you walk up to our humble dwellings, Lampwort?' probably gave it away.

'Good to see you again – Kenya seems so far away now,' Theodore said, shaking Lambert's hand.

'The other side of the world, my friend,' Lambert replied, not skipping a beat. 'How are you?' He seemed happy to be outside

and no longer cooped up in his luxury coach. Ever the gracious hostess, Bonnie brought glasses of lemonade out to the travellers, but Anya took one sip and exclaimed it wasn't cold enough. 'It's probably not what you're used to,' Bonnie replied carefully with a strained smile. 'I'll see what I can do.'

As Lambert instructed the driver to open up the back and fetch the presents, Theodore inched between him and the children.

'So good of you to come, Lambert – and the presents! There was no need; even the twins – that's overdoing it,' he chided.

'They're all Kingsleys,' the Viscount replied. 'Franklin would not have disapproved.'

'So nice to meet your wife,' Theodore said. 'Anya, isn't it? Forgive me for asking, but why is it Anya Stitz, and not Anya Knútr?'

'She won't allow it,' Lambert explained. 'She doesn't want to be a Knútr, but prefers her maiden name Stitz. It's a statement.'

Theodore blinked in surprise.

'After all, I prefer Lambert to Lamprecht,' he continued. 'I think it's good to make your own way in life.'

'Makes perfect sense to me,' Bea said crisply, catching Theodore's eye. 'Don't you think so, Carter?'

Cash broke the tension. 'Will you be staying with us, Lamstead? We have a guest room in the ranch.'

'You must call me Lambert,' said the Viscount. 'Thank you for your offer. Fortunately for us, the Pickwick Nite Coach offers us everything we need: bedrooms, bathrooms, even a lavatory. It is a mobile home in every sense.'

Anya, who was answering all of the twins' questions, saw them and floated away from the other children with a polite smile. 'Darling,' she purred, 'your special gift to Beatrice.'

Lambert smiled, and, like magic, from under his arm he produced a battered book. 'Your father's journal from Aru,' he announced.

'Oh gosh!' exclaimed Bea, her eyes lighting up with delight.

She reached out for it, but to her surprise Theodore took it from Lambert's hand. 'I think it's best if I look at it first,' he said.

Bea stared at him, stunned. 'Theodore, give it to me! Why should you take it?' She could feel hot rage welling up in her at Theodore's actions.

'Bea, I need to read it and make sure it's . . . suitable,' said Theodore firmly.

'I've read the first journal from Aru, and all the others in Father's library, so why not this one?' Bea demanded.

Lambert stepped in, announcing, 'I've read it and there's nothing in there that will scare her or could be considered inappropriate.'

'Thank you, Lambert,' Theodore said tersely, 'but as

her guardian I'll be the judge of that.' Turning to Bea, he told her, 'As soon as I've read it and approved it, you can have it.' He tried to sound reassuring, but it was clear from Bea's expression that it was not successful.

'Grandma would never have been so harsh!' burst out Bea, completely frustrated, and getting angrier by the second.

'That may be why you're so used to getting your way, young lady,' said Theodore sternly.

There was an uncomfortable silence at this angry exchange. The tension in the air was palpable. Lambert and Anya exchanged a glance, the corners of Anya's mouth turning up a fraction of a degree.

'Give it to me. It's rightfully mine,' Bea persisted.

'I'm only thinking of you,' repeated Theodore. 'All I want to do is check it out first in case there's anything that could be upsetting.'

'That's for me to decide, not you!' snapped Bea. 'That's my father's journal!'

'Bea, you've had a tough time lately –' began Theodore, but Bea cut him off.

'I'm fed up with you telling me what

I can and can't do!' she cried. 'You're not my parent!'

With that she spun on her heel and stormed off. Theodore stood there, journal in hand, helplessly watching her go.

'Listen, everyone,' Cash said, trying to diffuse the tension, 'why don't we all take a look in Lamebrat's coach? Apparently it has a toilet in it.'

Anya quickly shook her head but no one noticed.

'Yes please!' Carter, May and Violet shouted in unison.

'Great! Come on, children – what are you waiting for?' shouted Cash.

'Wonderful,' announced Lambert, who tried to smile at his wife, but she froze it off his face.

Carter and the girls were chattering excitedly at the prospect of seeing inside the glamorous vehicle as they passed Bea, who, following her outburst, was sitting in silent misery on the porch.

'You gotta come with us, Bea!' called Violet. 'We're going to see inside the Pickwick!'

'Bea,' Theodore said softly, approaching her. 'I'm sorry –'

But Bea turned her back on him and ran off to join her cousins.

Lambert saw the unhappy expression on Theodore's face and said, 'I can assure you, my friend, there's nothing in the journal except Franklin's mumbo jumbo about the Saurmen.'

Theodore heard the words and froze before finding his way back into the conversation. 'That mumbo jumbo represents the very last words her father wrote just before he was killed. That's got to be distressing on its own,' he said. He looked at the book, then asked, 'How did you get hold of it, Lambert? You said that when the raptors killed Grace and Franklin you were in such a bad state that you barely made it out of the jungle.'

The Viscount nodded. 'Yes, but in my delirium I grabbed what I thought was my own bag, and when I got back to the village I discovered I'd picked up Franklin's bag instead. I never found out what happened to my bag.' He pointed to the battered book in Theodore's hand. 'Actually I'm curious,' he added, 'Bea mentioned more journals?'

'Franklin always kept journals. They read half like a diary and half like a fairy tale. Some days he wrote everything; then there were some days, even weeks, when he wrote nothing. They're all a bit disjointed. They're all back in England.'

'I hope you don't mind that I read this diary,' Lambert said. 'I guess I was curious after all that happened on Aru, and I never expected to meet Franklin's family.'

They both looked to where the children were having a great time leaning out of the top windows of the Pickwick, while Cash had his head under the bonnet looking at the engine.

'I don't think he likes me,' said Lambert ruefully.

'Oh, Cash will warm to you,' Theodore assured him. 'He . . . he just thinks you could have found or contacted us, you know, in those eleven years.'

'He's right, of course,' Lambert said. 'I have had to learn to live with my mistakes, as they won't go away. There are so many things I wish I had done differently. I could have stopped all this before it started, and Franklin would be here with his children now. It's all my fault.'

Theodore patted the Viscount on the back. 'You're not to blame. We all have a past that haunts us. Come, let's have a drink,' he said kindly.

◆ ◆ ◆

Bonnie cooked up a feast and they all sat round in the dining room, which only got used for special occasions, generally a poker game on a Friday night with Cash's buddies.

'Mrs Kingsley, that was the most wonderful home-cooked food I have had in years – you really have a talent,' the Viscount said.

Bonnie blushed. 'Please,' she said, 'it's Bonnie, and it's a pleasure to serve you. Breakfast will be super-early tomorrow, remember, as we can't be late for the county fair!'

'So looking forward to it, and thank you again. Goodnight.'

Theodore followed Bonnie in to the kitchen. 'Bonnie, that was –' he began, but before he could say the rest she cut in.

'Stop right there,' she said, flicking a tea towel at him. 'You know what you have to do.'

Theodore tried again. 'But –'

'But nothing. Go and see Bea. You two need to make up; you can't sleep on bad feelings.'

'But –' he sputtered again.

'Go,' Bonnie said firmly, pointing to the door.

Bea was sitting alone on the porch, watching the day fade into night, when Theodore came and sat beside her.

'Sorry I messed up your last practice,' he said softly, 'and sorry I got cross about the journal.'

She stayed silent.

'Look,' he explained, 'we've been over this before: Bunty left it to me to look after you both.'

'She should have left it to *me* to look after you both,' Bea responded sourly. 'Let's face it, I would do a much better job.'

Bea had a smart answer for practically everything, but she and Theodore both knew this was probably true.

'Let me rephrase that,' Theodore clarified. 'Bunty wanted me to keep you out of trouble.'

But Bea had a good answer for that as well. 'The riding and the journal can't possibly get me into trouble,' she said in a hurt voice.

'Okay then, Bunty wanted me to keep you out of danger.'

'Riding Buster isn't dangerous – you're just scared. I don't see *you* doing tricks on saurs,' she spat.

'Hang on, young lady.' Theodore stood and waved a finger at her. 'Buster is a tyrant and you should never forget that. He was trained to do very bad things on Aru by that brute Christian Hayter. He's not like a tame allosaur.' Theodore tried to rise above his temper and keep focused on Bonnie's advice to patch things up, so he softened his tone a little. 'I've ridden almost every kind of saur, and tritops are for the ones who are definitely not scared. I've done my time in the rodeo.'

'Don't we know it! You're always bragging.' Bea crossed her arms. 'But reading can't possibly be dangerous. My father and mother *believed* in something,' she continued, 'and they must have talked to you about it. They travelled across the world and wrote it all down. I've read all the journals up to this one and there must be a reason why they went to Aru – can't you see that? Carter and I deserve to know!'

Theodore was taken aback. 'That's enough of this crazy talk,' he said firmly. 'You can ride in the fair tomorrow – do whatever you want – but please take extra care with Buster.' He held up a finger. 'And you can have a look at the journal after I've read it. But let's be crystal clear about one thing: Franklin and Grace left their loving family and friends to look for something that probably does not exist, then died a terrible death because of it.'

Bea gulped.

'And that was just the start of our problems. It's because of all that that Bunty died at the hands of that treacherous man we met on Aru,' he added.

Bea's eyes filled with tears. 'But we found Carter,' she reminded him.

Theodore looked to the sky and sighed. He put his arm round her shoulder. 'Can we just say sorry and forget about all this? You have a big day tomorrow and I want you to do your best and show them all how good you are,' he said warmly. 'Do it for Bunty.'

Despite herself, Bea couldn't bear to remain angry with Theodore. He looked so worried about her. Perhaps he was right, and it didn't mean anything. But she needed to believe that her parents hadn't died for a wild-goose chase.

7

The County Fair

~ a very strange feeling ~

The day started as promised, very early. Cash and Theodore got the trailer out, loaded the allosaurs, and woke Carter, who was found in the stable with Buster. The tyrant would have to run alongside, as the trailer wasn't big enough for both him and the allosaurs. The twins and Bea were all sharing a room, so were up and wearing their matching outfits by the time Bonnie called them for breakfast.

'Should I wake them?' Bonnie asked Bea as she looked out of the window at the Pickwick coach, whose curtains were still drawn. The driver was in a small canvas tent outside with his feet sticking out one end.

'I'd have found a bed for the poor man, if I'd known,' she declared. 'I assumed he had a bedroom in the coach.'

'Apparently they had it converted; it usually sleeps sixteen but it only fits two now,' Bea confirmed. 'Give me a tray and I'll take it to them.'

'And tell them they'll have to meet us there, as we leave in ten minutes,' Bonnie added.

♦ ♦ ♦

As soon as they arrived at the fair, the twins grabbed Bea's hand and eagerly darted off to check in and find out what slot they had in the day's entertainment. Carter, still on Buster's back, had a good vantage point and was taking it all in. There were a lot of cows in pens, and even more pens full of tritops, all with different horn and frill variations. There was a pen full of different hadros looking hot as a boy hosed them down, a substitute for their morning soak in a lake or river. Mimusaurs and some other odd-looking bipeds shared an enclosure with some kylos.

'Excuse me, sir.' A young man in a Stetson hat came up to Theodore. 'What kind of saur is that?' He pointed at Buster.

'Mighty fine, isn't he?' Theodore said proudly. 'He's a Black Dwarf Tyrant.'

'Why ain't it shackled?' the man nervously replied.

'He doesn't need to be,' Theodore assured him. 'He's tame.'

The man took his hat off and wiped his brow with his sleeve. 'But tyrants can't be tamed – they're savages!'

'I can assure you he's –'

'You should shackle it, sir. This is a family event; my children are here,' the man protested, cutting Theodore off, before putting his hat back on and walking off.

'How rude,' Theodore muttered to himself as Carter slid down from Buster's back.

'Why the cages?' Carter tugged at Theodore's shirt and pointed to a line of metal cages, some large enough for a

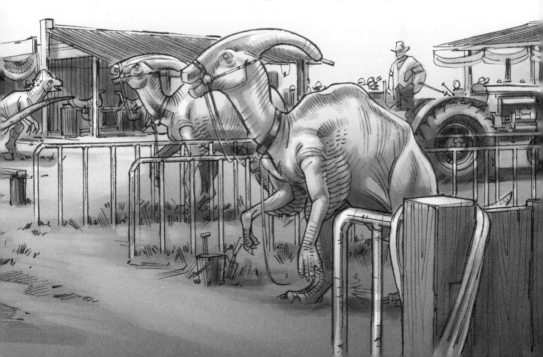

human, going down to ones the size of a shoebox, which housed a variety of smaller creatures. Carter did not like the look of this, as it reminded him of his brief time spent caged up at the hands of Christian Hayter back in Aru.

'They're just for transportation,' Theodore explained, 'like Cash's trailer for the allos, and then for displaying them for a competition. They're probably well looked after and run free back where they come from.'

Cash and Bonnie returned from greeting people with troubled looks on their faces. 'There are a lot of unhappy people out there,' Cash said, shaking his head.

'Looks like we've been the lucky ones. Putting our saurs in the paddocks at night has probably saved us; those who can't do that have all been attacked several times,' Bonnie explained.

'And no one knows what's been mutilating them?' Theodore asked.

'That's the strangest part – all the accounts are slightly different; some people have even heard strange noises and seen lights glowing on the horizon at night,' said Cash, puzzled.

May, Violet and Bea bounded over, full of excitement with news of their upcoming performance. 'Good news! Our closest rivals, the Crossley Boys, have dropped out,' said May.

'Two of them got trampled in practice yesterday,' added Violet, before realising that Bea was shaking her head and mouthing 'No, no, no' behind Theodore. 'They're . . . not hurt or anything, just bruises . . .' she trailed off.

May, who had not yet seen Bea's silent warning, corrected her sister. 'And a broken leg,' she added.

Theodore grimaced and looked at Bea with concern.

'You should sign up for the rodeo,' Bea suggested pointedly. 'There are still some open slots.'

It was a challenge, and Theodore knew it. 'I think I just might, young lady,' he said.

◆ ◆ ◆

The county fair was packed with people enjoying the amusements, the rides, the stalls and the entertainers. Cash took Theodore, Lambert and Anya on a tour down one avenue of new mechanical farming machinery being shown off to prospective clients, but everyone seemed to be looking and not buying.

'Things are still tough,' Cash explained. 'People just don't have the savings and the banks don't lend any more. You mentioned that you had some business interests around here, Lankbert,' he added. 'What are they?'

'I'm looking at a factory, to expand one of my business,' replied Lambert non-committally.

Cash nodded, wondering which factory he could be talking about, but let it go.

Carter lagged behind, and gazed intently at all the livestock. There was an area for exotic animals, and one proud rancher had ostriches all the way over from Australia.

'I know what you're thinking,' the man said to Carter. 'This ain't a saur; it's a bird!'

Carter was confused. Its eggs were exactly the same as a mimus's.

There was a lonely stytops, though not a red one like he knew from Africa; this one was brown with paler patches and had short frill horns. One man was giving a falconry display, but the falcon in question had flown off and had not returned, which put a smile on Carter's face.

The main attractions were the performances and rodeo in the main arena, an oval construction of whitewashed wooden high fences adorned with red, white and blue bunting and garlands. Behind this were two raised sets of bench seats – bleachers, they called them, because the people sitting on them baked in the sun – and a larger covered stand for special guests next to a booth where the announcements were made. A board displayed the names of the events, with the rides and times next to them.

The arena was already packed with people, so Carter climbed up a telegraph pole to get a good view. The lucky ones had managed to grab seats early, but everyone else seemed happy enough to lean against the white wooden boards around the arena and peer in through the open sections, or sit on a bale of straw.

'Ladies and gentlemen,' the announcer boomed, 'now for the synchronised performances.' The crowd applauded as Bea, May and Violet trotted into the arena through the large wooden gate that led out to the back.

'As you know, we don't run these performances as a competition, but all the talented young people taking part today take it very seriously. This year we will therefore be judging this by your applause. Whoever gets the most applause will take home the People's Choice Award.'

Bea and the twins looked to each other and winked.

'First up, three young ladies who show no fear – it's the Kingsley Cousin Riders. And yes, ladies and gentlemen, that large black saur ain't no allosaur; it's . . . Hang on, have you got this right, Bob?' The commentator fumbled with his paperwork and got confirmation as to what was written in front of him. 'Well, if you say so, Bob . . . Ladies and gentlemen, for the first time ever at our county fair, we have a tyrant with us: a Black Dwarf from Flores.'

The audience gasped and Bea looked around nervously. May and Violet were each holding one arm high with a wide performer's smile, so she joined in.

'One, two, three, go!' May said under her breath.

Everything went according to plan, and once all three were riding in a perfect circle and at speed, they started to climb and slide to the side of their saurs. The audience swelled as word got out that a tyrant was performing, and the 'oooohs' and 'aaaahs' from the crowd grew as each turn and trick grew more dangerous.

The girls needed every bit of concentration to keep their balance, keep time, and remember each move.

The three-way criss-cross and interchange – the most difficult manoeuvre – went with balletic ease. The crowd roared their appreciation.

Carter joined in and whistled loudly as every eye was fixed on the triumphant spectacle before them. Then he suddenly got a very strange feeling. A cold chill in the heat of the day ran down his spine and the hairs on the back of his neck prickled. He tried to sniff out trouble, but got a mix of candyfloss and hot dogs instead. He looked around from his vantage point but could see nothing unusual.

Then Carter heard the crowd gasp. He looked frantically into the arena to see May and Violet going around together, but Buster and Bea were a heap in the dust.

8

The Terrible Tyrant

~ an object of curiosity ~

Buster had suddenly frozen on the spot and then fallen hard to the ground, to everyone's shock. Bea had managed to cling on and was now being hoisted back up again, holding on to his neck feathers for dear life. Carter scrambled down from the telegraph pole and into the ring.

Buster frantically tried to shake Bea off while May and Violet took a wider circle away from Buster and slowed down. As usual, the allosaurs had blinkers on to shield them from any sudden movements to the side, so keeping them turning and away from Buster was a good idea.

'This isn't part of the routine,' Bonnie said, then gulped as she held her hands over her eyes and peered through her fingers. Anya, sitting beside her, looked on without emotion while wafting the smell from the livestock away with her lace fan. The audience reflected Bonnie's concern, gasping with every jolt and flick of Buster's tail.

The tyrant's huge head swung from side to side with such force that the reins made to fit over the bridge of his snout and under his chin whipped Bea like a rag doll. She realised that letting go would mean a long drop and probably broken bones, if she was lucky. Holding on until Buster stopped was her only option. As the tyrant tired slightly and the twists and jolts became less frequent, she managed to swing herself back into position just behind his shoulders.

She saw Carter waving madly, trying to get Buster in front of him, but the beast was still enraged. Theo was right, she admitted to herself reluctantly.

Carter was desperate. Buster didn't usually act this way. He could tell that the tyrant had been spooked by the same thing that he'd felt. He looked up again, but Buster was too deranged to notice him.

The sheriff looked to his to deputies, who had joined him at the side of the announcer's booth. 'If that girl don't get that tyrant under control, boys, you'll have to shoot, got it?'

They both nodded.

'Should never have brought a tyrant here, a vicious saur like that. Where's Cash Kingsley?'

One deputy pointed to the VIP stand.

'Train your rifles on that monster,' the sheriff growled. 'I'm going to have a word.'

✦ ✦ ✦

Buster crouched down and then leapt violently off the ground with such force that Bea's hand slipped from the reins, sending her forward and grabbing at his neck.

With another jolt she slipped and swung round to the side of Buster's neck, pulling hard on his feathers to stop herself from falling. Suddenly Buster paused. Bea had her moment, and pulled herself up by holding on tight to a clump of feathers, as Buster winced in pain. It was enough to make him suddenly snap out of his crazed state.

'There, there,' she said. 'It's over now.'

✦ ✦ ✦

The sheriff had reached Cash, who was sitting next to Lambert up in the shaded VIP seats. 'This is a family event, Cash,' he said hotly. 'What're you doing bringing a wild tyrant here? That thing's out of control!'

'Don't know what you're talking about, Sheriff,' replied Cash.

'Why, it's just an act; there's no way my friend here would endanger people,' said Lambert politely.

The sheriff turned to the ring. To his amazement, Bea was now sitting still on Buster's back, patting him gently.

✦ ✦ ✦

A huge wave of relief came over Bea, but the ordeal was far from over. Her cousins were still galloping around and the crowd looking on intently. When they could see that Buster was back under control, the twins closed in towards Bea as per their original routine, and flanked Buster on both sides.

May and Violet counted out the end part of the routine so that they were perfectly in time. 'One, two, three, hands out; one, two, three, hand up.'

Bea did not attempt to join in, but simply held on to the reins tightly and clenched Buster's sides with her knees.

When they exited the arena, the ranch hands took the allosaurs while Theodore and Carter grabbed on to Buster. Behind them, the crowd was too stunned to do much more than clap, and whisper about what they had just witnessed. One minute it was an amazing spectacle; the next it was the most frightening thing anyone had seen – then suddenly it was all over.

'Bea, you held on and rode magnificently,' Theodore said with relief.

'You're cross with me, I know,' she said.

The twins ran over and patted her on the shoulders. 'We thought you were a gonner out there,' gasped May.

'You ride better than the men in the rodeo!' gushed Violet.

But Bea was too distraught to hear their compliments. 'Listen to the crowd,' Bea sobbed. 'They all saw; it was a complete disaster. I'm sorry I failed. I should never have spoiled your perfect routine.'

Bonnie ran up and immediately took Bea for a warm cuddle. 'Come here now, Bea, you're alive, and, if I may say, one heck of a saur rider!'

Cash patted her on the back. 'Your father would have

been proud of the way you brought Buster back under control, girl, mighty proud.'

It was small consolation to Bea, however, who felt silly for not taking Theodore's advice.

Lambert and Anya made their way over. 'Carter, your sister deserves a medal for bravery; that certainly was an ordeal,' the Viscount said.

Theodore could see people were staring at them, and not in a good way. He pointed to where the others had gone and told Lambert they would join him later once they had Buster sorted out.

'Look, Carter, you're not going to like this, but we need to put Buster in a pen and shackle him. It's for his own safety,' said Theodore with a heavy heart.

Carter's eyes welled up with tears but he nodded reluctantly.

Buster shackled in a pen became an object of curiosity. Carter leant against the bars, unable to bear leaving him. People crowded around. Everyone wanted to come and see the vicious terrible tyrant that had put on such a spectacle.

9

The Cockney Cowboy

~ a load of mumbo jumbo ~

'Ladies and gentlemen,' the announcer boomed, 'we welcome you back to the arena for our main event: the rodeo. I can't guarantee it will be as thrilling and dangerous as this morning's unusual performance by the Kingsley Cousin Riders. A teenage girl lasting four minutes on a crazed tyrant! By the way, what was that girl's name, Bob? . . . Beatrice Kingsley, a newcomer to the sport and all the way from . . . What does that say, Bob? That can't be right . . . Heck, if any one of you tough men out there can last longer on a small old tritops than a little girl from England, then I'll eat my hat.'

'That was the best trick-riding I've ever seen,' enthused one elderly man when he saw Bea, 'and I've been coming to the county fair for years!'

'Especially when you pretended you were going to fall,' chuckled his companion. 'You had me worried for a second. I kept telling them it was all part of the show, but the people around me were gasping, I tell ya.'

'Thank you,' smiled Bea.

Violet whispered to her cousin, 'Told you they'd think it was part of the act.'

'And now . . .!' boomed the announcer. 'It's our own local bull tritops champion – please give a big hand to Pete Knight!'

The crowd cheered. Bea looked over to where a young handsome man was standing atop the chute that would drop him onto a huge bull tritops waiting below.

The ropes holding the tritops were released; the gate was opened; and the man was out, holding on grimly as the saur leapt up and down, jerking left and right, its massive head lowered, then raised in a desperate effort to unseat the man on its back. The tritops charged round the arena, kicking up dust, then skidded to a sudden halt, throwing Pete Knight forward and smashing him against its bony neck frill. It wasn't long before he was hurled into the air and crashed down. Immediately the rodeo clowns ran to his aid, the brightly dressed men dancing and distracting the tritops while others ran to the motionless rider. They clumsily picked him up, then dropped him, so opted to half drag him to a waiting stretcher. The tritops took some time to realise it was relieved of its burden, and settled itself down enough to be led out of the arena.

'Folks, give a big hand for our current winner at twelve seconds, Pete Knight. Let's hope he recovers from that fall, or it will be goodnight to the Knight!' The crowd laughed.

'Who's up next? Thanks, Bob. And now, folks, someone who's returned to these shores after many years away. Please let's give a big hand to Theodore Logan, the Cockney Cowboy!'

Bea felt her stomach sink. Now that she'd had a taste of how truly dangerous it could be in the ring, she wished she hadn't urged Theodore to sign up. What if he got injured . . . or worse? Bea would never forgive herself.

Cash patted his old friend on the back for good luck as Theodore balanced, legs astride at the top of the short chute – then, at a wave from the timekeeper – he slid down, landing in the saddle and grabbing the reins. Immediately the gate opened and the tritops leapt out, bucking furiously, determined to get rid of this weight on its back. Theodore held on, gripping tight with his knees and ankles, keeping the reins short.

'Oh my goodness, he's actually doing it!' Bea gasped, barely able to look.

Within a second, Theodore felt every part of his body ache as the tritops hurled itself into the air, then crashed down, lifting him up and slamming him down onto the saddle. As he hung on, knees still tightly gripping the huge saur, it shook hard from side to side, trying to throw him off, but he was expecting it and went with the movement. It wasn't just his body on the line;

it was his pride. By taking up Bea's challenge Theodore hoped to prove to her he was still a force to be reckoned with, someone deserving of respect. He realised that if he failed, he'd have a harder time than ever of getting back on level ground with her. It hit him that as much as they had tried to pretend everything was normal, they were all still grieving – the children perhaps less able to hide it than him.

As this occurred to Theodore, his flailing hand brushed against the knife on his belt, and he felt the keystone set into the hilt. A surge shot through him like nothing he'd ever felt before. Theodore remembered the Saurman's wise words and suddenly the whole arena seemed silent and motionless. He was still completely conscious and alert, yet his eyes were fixed, his body slightly raised from being bucked upwards, making him feel weightless. He could even feel his hair standing on end.

Theodore was frozen in time, and so was everything around him – yet here he was, awake in a single moment. Even though he looked forward, he could see himself above the tritops. He could feel the animal beneath him, its heart caught mid-beat. He could feel that it was uncomfortable and distressed. He could even feel a rusty nail lodged between two toes on its back foot that was adding to its burden. The palm of his hand was connected to the keystone, opening up all of his five senses and making him hyper-sensitive to everything around him. Then Theodore felt his eyelids become increasingly heavy and slowly lower past his fixed view like heavy metal shutters being wound down.

Then, after what felt like ages, Theodore blinked, and it was all over.

The tritops bucked violently, sending Theodore flying. He slammed hard onto the dry dusty ground behind it. There he lay for a few moments gathering himself together. Whatever happened just then was what he had been hoping to find for years: some sort of sign or proof that this was not all a load of mumbo jumbo.

All his senses were still energised. Not only could Theodore sense behind him the tritops pad around and lift its back foot to alleviate the pain of the nail wedged in it, but he could also feel the relief that it no longer had him on top. He could taste the dirt mixing with blood from his lip. He could smell all the individual aromas in the air. He could hear everyone in the crowd roar as the clowns waved the tritops away from him. He could feel the footsteps of the ranch hands and the rough rope in their hands ready to lasso the tritops and secure it. He looked into the crowd of people and could see Carter and Bea staring right back at him.

Suddenly everything was crystal clear, and he knew what Kunava in Aru had been trying to tell him, and what the Stegosorcerer's words of wisdom all meant.

He understood that his and Carter's paths in life were the same: two children orphaned and raised by saurs, then saved by two special people and given a chance at a completely different future. It was like they were twins separated by a generation, two halves of the same thing. And there was Bea, who was protecting them both and helping him unlock this faith, forcing Theodore to address his fears and not be scared to trust all that he feared to be true.

For the first time in Theodore's life he knew exactly what he had to do: find the truth about the keystone and go back to the sacred temple tree in Aru. The answers he sought would be there. Then he remembered what else the Stegosorcerer had said: that the bad man's path also ran with his, and that he would see Christian Hayter again. He shivered involuntarily.

Theodore leapt to his feet and dusted himself down, feeling for broken bones. He turned to the ranch hands who had lassoed the tritops and were pulling it, took the rope from them, and let it drop to the floor. He walked up to one of the clowns who was waving his oversized gloves at the tritops, pulled off his bright wig and false nose, and gestured for them both to push off.

He was left face to face with the bull tritops in front of him and the ranch hands looking on in confusion. He turned back to the large tritops who was still panting heavily from the ordeal, and looked straight at it. He patted it on the nose horn with one hand and stroked its face with the other. It didn't flinch. Everyone in the crowd held their breath. Theodore continued to stare deep into the tritops' eyes, then man and saur both blinked at the same time. Theodore took a deep breath, sighed, and said. 'Sorry.'

He then walked round to the saur's back leg and bent down to look at his large toes. One of the ranch hands walked over, but he was pushed aside by Cash.

'You all right, Theo?' he asked.

Theodore looked back at him with a newfound clarity in his eyes. 'This tritops has something wedged in its toe causing some pain – help me lift it.'

Cash leant in to the tritops, who was still amazingly still for a saur who only moments ago had been bucking Theodore about wildly.

Cash took the tritops's foot and tugged it upwards to reveal the padded underside. 'You're right; it's swelled up with some sort of splinter,' he said.

Theodore gently ran his hand all the way down the passive tritops' leg to its foot and lightly made his way over the swelling, where there was something sticking out caked in blood and dirt. He looked to Cash who was outwardly calm, but also aware that a thousand-odd people were watching them intently. Theodore gently held the end and pulled it out in one fluid move. The tritops flinched but immediately calmed. Cash let go and

it rested its foot back to the ground. It snorted and called out with a satisfying *wharrrr*.

'Dang, that's a big rusty nail. Gotta hurt,' said Cash. 'How did you know?'

Theodore stood and patted the docile tritops on the back. 'I just knew,' he said.

10

Christian Hayter

~ that horrid little man ~

The Pickwick coach made its way up the long dirt road that ran alongside the railway line and up to the closed slaughterhouse on the Peabody estate. It was hot and the air was thick with a shimmering haze.

The slaughterhouse was perfectly situated to accommodate all the ranchers who raised livestock and had been running a fair business until the water dried up. It was built beside the train line and had several sidings

where freight could be loaded to make its way around the country in refrigerated carriages. Surrounding it were large pens that could hold the livestock awaiting slaughter and small buildings for goods and accommodation. The place was empty of any life except for one long black train that was parked up in a siding where some people were milling around the carriages at the rear.

'Looks like the boss is here – don't stand about, make yourself look useful,' Christian Hayter barked at his accomplices, Mr Ash and Mr Bishop. They did as they were told and started to lower the wooden ramp from the side of the open train carriage to the ground as the Pickwick pulled in.

The driver parked, then ran round and opened the door for the Viscount who stepped out into the sunlight.

'Would you get a parasol for my wife? The sun is too harsh for her at this time of day,' he called to the driver as he walked over to where Hayter was waiting. 'Is the owner's land agent here yet?' the Viscount asked.

'Yes, he's with our surveyor looking over the place now. Been here for an hour almost – they should be back soon,' Hayter replied.

'Good.'

Anya Stitz emerged from the coach in a white silk outfit fitted with a long draping cape and a hat perfectly placed at a fashionable angle. Ash and Bishop stopped what they were doing and stared.

Anya paused to take in the long black train, Hayter, and the men dithering about in the background. She turned to the empty landscape stretching as far as the eye could see, then to the slaughterhouse boarded up with a 'KEEP OUT' sign chained over the entrance. She turned back to her husband, who was grinning. She glared at him, then headed back into the Pickwick coach, all under the shade of the driver's umbrella. Before she slammed the door, she called behind her, 'Tell me when this trip becomes interesting, and make it fast.'

The Viscount sighed deeply, then turned to Hayter once more. 'So have you acquainted yourself with the Doctor yet, Mr Hayter?'

Hayter tried to look busy, then turned to answer the question. 'He keeps himself to himself down in his laboratory carriages most of the day, then heads out at night. I head him say something about a county fair.'

'He did, did he? I thought as much. He's probably curious to see the livestock and is up to his old tricks again.' The Viscount looked up the length of the customised train. 'I figured it was his handiwork that made your old black tyrant go berserk. Caused quite a spectacle. Sadly it did not win the People's Choice Award – that was given to an old man who had a singing donkey. Much safer than a rampant tyrant, and quite comical.' He smiled. 'Perhaps next year for the Kingsley cousins, though I doubt it,' he mused.

'*My* black tyrant?' Hayter spat. 'The Beast is here in America?'

'Yes. But probably not for long – its days are numbered thanks to the Doctor's handiwork. They've had to have it shackled, and soon enough people will be blaming it for all the mutilations. By the way, do we have an update on that?'

'I think the Doctor wants to report to you personally,' Hayter responded. 'He had a little trouble.'

'How much trouble?'

'Think he wanted to tell you himself.'

'*Tell me,*' the Viscount commanded.

'He lost a tyrant.' Hayter shrugged as if it was nothing much.

'*What!* How did this happen?'

'Several days ago we stopped along the line – the

driver needed to check the pressure or oil – anyway, one of the Doctor's men went to check on the pack and never came back. So the Doctor went over with the other chap and found him – well, half of him. He got cross at the tyrants; was shouting in German at them and everything. We heard it all up this end.'

'Then what?'

'Well, that's it – we have no idea what he did, but they all went crazy in the carriage. Tore it to bits, they did. That's when the other chap who works for him got a bit too close, apparently. By the time we got there, there wasn't much we could do except uncouple the carriage that was torn apart and burn it – you know, to cover our tracks. Didn't want to have to explain how a man died.'

'Wise move; you did well.'

'Anyway, the Doctor was still cursing – seems like one went missing. It must have scarpered in the mayhem. But by then it was long gone; nothing we could do about it.'

The Viscount took a deep breath and curled his face into a pained expression. 'Thank you, Mr Hayter, for telling me,' he said, brushing some dust from his sleeve.

'So now we're here, what can we do for you?' asked Hayter.

The Viscount looked the slaughterhouse over. 'I had in mind for you a task well suited to your talents –' he gestured to the empty building – 'namely, being the boss of this place.'

Hayter cracked a smile.

'You proved yourself in Africa, after messing up in Aru, that is. And I had visions of you running my new North American operations.'

Hayter's smile grew into a huge grin.

'However, it sounds like the Doctor is behind schedule. He's missing a tyrant, skipping work to cause mischief at county fairs, and now is suddenly very short-staffed. So I will need you to help him.'

Hayter's face dropped. 'What?'

'He has very important work to do and I can't have any more mishaps or delays,' the Viscount explained.

'But I don't want to work for him,' Hayter barked.

'You're very much mistaken, Mr Hayter,' the Viscount said icily. 'You work for me, and have done since the very day I dragged you out of the raptor pits in London. The Doctor also works for me, and so do those useless men over there.' He jabbed a finger at Ash and Bishop. 'This big lump of black metal is mine.' He gestured down the length of the train. 'Soon this slaughterhouse will be mine and all the ranches around here, one by one, all *mine*.' He paused. 'So let's make this simple for you to understand. When I tell you what to do, you do it. You don't whine and complain; you just do it.'

'But this is all the Doctor's fault,' uttered Hayter petulantly.

The Viscount held up his walking cane threateningly.

'I'll deal with the Doctor in my own time. However, I appreciate you alerting me to what's going on behind my back. Please continue to do so. Information is crucial. In fact, that's why I'm placing you with him. Trust me, there is a lot you could learn from that man. Plus, I need you to keep tabs on him; he has a tendency to . . . go off the rails, lose focus. If this happens, you come to me – not with any of your petty issues, like who has the bigger carriage on this train. Big issues, ones that affect my business. You understand, Mr Hayter?'

'Yes, boss,' Hayter grunted.

'Sorry . . . what was that?' The Viscount stared at him.

'Pardon me, yes, Viscount, sir!' Hayter pulled upright like a soldier and almost saluted.

'And get those two fools working for a change.' The Viscount waved at Ash and Bishop with his cane and set off to the slaughterhouse, where two men had appeared from a doorway and were talking in the sunshine.

'So, what do you think?' the Viscount asked the surveyor.

'Looks like they left the place in good condition and you won't have to do much to modernise it,' said the surveyor.

'How much do they want for the place?'

'Half of what they originally wanted,' said the man in the suit, eager to close the deal on behalf of the owner. 'Probably a good time to buy, I would say.'

The Viscount sniffed. 'No – it's not worth even half. I'll pay the real cost of this worthless place,' he said. 'The Great Depression has made everyone desperate. Let's see if they get any other buyers; I hear everyone is in the same boat . . . except me.'

'Don't leave it too long,' the surveyor advised, 'the land is used to reclaiming what's built on it. There ain't much left of the old mining town over yonder. Of course, you do know that you'll have to dig your own well for water, or pipe it in from elsewhere, which will be costly. There's a real shortage around here. The old supply to this place dried up, and won't come back; that's what forced them to shut up shop in the first place.'

The Viscount sneered. 'They should be paying me to take this burden from them. Tell the owners . . . my last offer – the *only* offer they will get for this "cursed" place – is for . . . one dollar.'

The land agent looked rattled.

'People around here depend on this place,' the Viscount continued, 'and I am their only saviour. Without this place, there are no jobs and no money in the town. Tell the owners that the burden they have will transfer to me, for a single dollar, and that is all. If they don't, I'll make sure their names are mud.'

The man nodded and gulped. 'I will try to persuade them, sir,' he said, and left.

Hayter had hung back and overheard what was said.

'But what about the water problem?' he asked.

'There is no problem, Mr Hayter,' the Viscount explained. 'I created the water shortage. It was to help the stupid owners of this place make the right decision to sell it to me for a cut price. The other ranchers will follow because they believe the land is somehow cursed. Their livestock is being torn to shreds by an unknown monster, and soon enough all the wells will run dry and the land will turn to dust. Without water, this part of the world is worthless.'

'Why do you want to buy worthless land?' Hayter asked, puzzled.

'Have you not been listening? It's not worthless at all. When I own it I will divert the water back.' The Viscount offered a slight smile. 'I already own the canning company, the products and the shipping company. Soon, one of those dozy tritops out there will be served on a plate somewhere in the world and I will have made a profit at every point along its journey. Now let's go and pay the Doctor a visit and get back to work,' the Viscount said, and turned on his heel, leaving Hayter staring after him with grudging admiration.

11

Red Water

~ something terrible ~

Bonnie put one of her mighty pies on the table and rang the big bell on the porch for dinner. She really didn't have to, as the delicious aroma was enough to lure everyone there from miles around. It was the perfect cure to brighten everyone's mood after the disastrous events of the previous day.

'Wash your hands in the bowl, please, children,' she instructed as they rushed in. 'The tap's not up to pressure again. Cash, would you be a dear and have a look later? It hasn't been good all day and the dishes will need doing.'

'Sure thing,' Cash replied, and gave his wife a kiss on the cheek and a quick squeeze.

Theodore noticed Bea and Carter staring.

'Come along now, you two,' he urged them, 'you've been in the paddock all day with the saurs – your hands need a good wash and you'll probably need a bath later.' He tried to hurry them into the kitchen but felt stiff and sore from his rodeo ride on the bull tritops.

'Were Mummy and Daddy like you and Cash?' Bea asked her aunt as she helped with the dinner.

'In many ways,' she replied. 'Cash was always more grounded and mature than Franklin, and Grace was just like Bunty, but more carefree, and together they were a great couple. They loved each other, and you, very much.'

'Me too?' Carter chirped up while tackling the soap.

'I'm sure of it,' Bonnie replied, going to dry her hands.

Bea looked across at Theodore and sighed. 'Violet and May are so lucky to have parents.'

'That they are,' Theodore agreed, dipping his hands into the water and grappling the soap from Carter. 'My mother died giving birth to me – I was never even held, you know.' He tried to offer a story worse than theirs to make things seem a bit better.

'But you had a father and brothers,' Bea pointed out.

'Indeed I did,' Theodore whispered, his heart heavy. He'd tried to talk to Bea about the journals once they returned from the fair, but she'd turned away each time.

'Sadly I don't think there'll be enough water for a bath later – the water's down to a trickle,' Bonnie said as her eye caught movement out of the window. 'Cash,' she hollered, 'Cody's outside to see you.'

'Hey, Cody, good to see you,' Cash said, as they shook hands on the porch.

'It's not good, Cash, none of it is.' His neighbour wore a concerned expression.

'What's troubling you, old friend?'

'My tritops was killed last night,' Cody told him.

'Sorry to hear that,' replied Cash. 'Whatever's doing this is a real problem.'

Theodore joined them. 'Evening, Cody – you all right? Looks like you've seen Old Man Peabody on the way here!'

'This ain't no laughing matter,' Cody said. 'My tritops is dead. But this time something's different. Whatever did it left footprints behind.'

Cash and Theodore leant in curiously. 'What kind of prints?' Cash asked.

Cody cleared his throat and spat in the dirt. 'A tyrant's.'

Cash shook his head. 'Can't be a tyrant – there aren't any about.'

'That so?' Cody said, putting his hands on his hips. 'Sure looked like a Black Tyrant causing a stir at the county fair the other day.' He looked around nervously. 'Please tell me it's shackled up and not loose on your ranch.'

Cash frowned. 'You know, he's actually my nephew's pet; he's harmless.'

'You expect me to believe that!' Cody spat. 'A pet tyrant! Who's your nephew, the King of England? I'm no fool!'

'Honestly, Cody, Buster's perfectly tame,' Theodore added.

'Funny how you're the only ranch around here not affected by the slaughterhouse closure,' Cody ventured, his tone now direct and somewhat sinister.

'You're right,' Cash replied testily. 'I've no interest in filling my land with cattle and tritops to fill the plates and stomachs of people in the city. Unlike you, Cody, I no longer profit from dead saurs.'

The air between the two men prickled with tension.

'For all we know, you could have switched from breeding

allosaurs to breeding tyrants, and that black one is a new exotic stud! How about reintroducing Mountain Tyrants as well?' Cody added, now that he was on a roll. 'There was a reason those monsters were wiped out by settlers long ago.'

Theodore stepped in. 'Why don't you come to the stables and meet Buster, Cody?' he offered. 'Carter can make him do a trick for you if you like.'

Cody gave Theodore a cold stare. 'Listen here,' he said coldly. 'I think we saw enough of its tricks yesterday. I'm trying to be a good friend and neighbour to you all, so if you know what's good for you, Logan, I'd leave and take that tyrant with you. I won't be able to stop the others when they come marching down here.' He turned to leave. 'You'd best heed my warning,' he said over his shoulder as he went.

A little while later Cash and Theodore sat down at the table, unsettled by the exchange. Everyone had already started and Bonnie handed them both plates.

'Is Buster in trouble again?' Carter asked worriedly.

Cash smiled back. 'No – it's just a misunderstanding,' he said, brushing Carter's ear playfully. 'Cody's a good man, just under a lot of pressure. You girls showed everyone how talented Buster was at the county fair and people take a long time to adjust to the changes going on around here. Trust me, these folks will respect and trust saurs again, you'll see.' He winked at the boy and plunged his fork into his pie.

After dinner the children got out board games and sat round the fire, while Cash went off to the well with his toolbox. Theodore cleared the table, and then showed Bonnie how he washed up during the war. This consisted of licking the plates clean, then dipping them in the dirty water they'd washed their hands in, before rubbing them with a clean towel. Bonnie smiled, but insisted on washing them once the water was back on.

'How is it back at home, Theo, without Bunty?' Bonnie asked while they did their best with the cutlery. 'I noticed things between you and Bea have been . . . tense.'

'It's been hard,' Theodore admitted. 'Bunty was the only sort of parent Bea knew, and, as you know, she spoilt that child rotten. As for Carter – well, he knew Bunty for such a short time, but it made a huge impression at a time when he was making the biggest adjustment of his life, stepping off that island, and stepping into the human race.' Theodore paused then continued, 'Then we went to Kenya and all that trouble. As if the boy hadn't been through enough.'

'And going to England must have been strange too?' Bonnie said.

Theodore nodded. 'Bunty's old house runs itself; the housekeeper and gardener look after it, but it's big and empty.' He paused. 'And don't ask about school,' he added, rolling his eyes. 'I mean – imagine returning to school after that rollercoaster of adventure and emotion.'

'I see,' Bonnie said. 'And you, Theo, how are you?'

Theodore dropped his gaze. Emotions weren't his thing, but they were firing all over the place.

'You don't know how good it is to be here amongst a real family again, for me and the children,' he choked out as his eyes welled up.

Bonnie gave him a hug. 'Now then,' she said softly, 'you know you're welcome to stay as long as you like. Don't let Cody scare you off. The children could even go to school here. Take your time, Theo, and settle back into normal life.'

The tap suddenly made a spluttering noise, and after a few spurts started to run freely.

'Good old Cash!' Bonnie exclaimed with a big smile. 'He can fix anything, you know!'

Theodore pulled himself together and took the stack of half-cleaned plates from the sideboard. He smiled back. 'Shall I wash everything properly this time?'

But as he dipped the plates into the sink he noticed something terrible.

The water didn't run clear; it ran red.

12

The Three-Way Split

~ where it all started ~

Cash, Bonnie and Theodore stood looking into the well.

'What's going on, Cash?' Theodore asked. 'Why is the water red all of a sudden?'

'I'm not sure,' Cash responded. 'The well here is dry, so I've been pumping water to it from another. The pressure's been weak for a few months and steadily getting worse. Now the spring's bringing up red water from somewhere.' Cash wiped his brow with his pocket scarf.

'Could Cody have done this?' suggested Theodore quietly.

Cash shook his head. 'Not likely.'

'Then who or what?' said Bonnie, troubled.

'Well, we all know it's not a stupid curse, but it's definitely something. I'll ride off first thing in the morning to check the springs further up in the hills where our water comes from. Until then, let's not startle the children. I'll turn this red water off at the well so no one sees it. Until it's fixed I have a few barrels in case of fires in the big barn.

They won't last long, so we'll have to ration it.'

Theodore nodded. 'I'll come with you.'

'No – Cody could come back. You'll need to stay.'

'What about Buster?' Theodore asked worriedly. 'If Cody's right, and everyone thinks he's responsible, there's not a lot I can do to stop them. Carter would be destroyed – and I can't risk that. It's taken me a long time to gain the boy's trust, and it's on thin ice now that I've had Buster penned up.'

Cash thought for a while. 'Carter and Buster could join me, and stay safely away from trouble in the mountains. It may take a few days, but hopefully we can solve this before we get blamed for it.'

Theodore considered Cash's plan before he reluctantly shook his head.

Bonnie suggested Cash take Buster alone, but Theodore knew Carter would refuse to be separated from his pet.

'I could take all the children shopping!' Bonnie said suddenly. 'That way, there's no one here using up the water and we're out of harm's way.'

'What?' blurted Cash and Theodore simultaneously.

'Lambert and Anya were planning on returning after their business meeting, so it would be a distraction for them too.' She was building up steam now. 'It's clear as day that Anya isn't happy being stuck out here in the countryside. She's a city girl and used to the finer things in life. And Lambert – well, he's interested in buying gifts. If I mentioned that I've been saving up to take the girls out to Sacramento, they won't be able to help themselves. I could suggest that we pop in to see a show and make an evening of it. We could make it last at least two days.'

Cash and Theodore glanced at each other, and then at Bonnie, who was twirling her toe in the dirt nonchalantly, a big grin on her face.

'Brilliant idea, Bonnie,' Theodore almost shouted, 'but how about San Francisco for three nights?' With that he ran into the house and grabbed his jacket off the coat hook. The children all turned round and gave him a funny look.

'Carry on,' he said hastily, 'don't mind me,' and dashed outside again as they went back to their game.

He rummaged around and found what he was looking for in one of his many pockets.

'Would these make a better excuse?' he said as he handed Bonnie a creased-up silver envelope that had already been opened. 'Tell them you're taking the children to the movies in San Francisco!' Theodore beamed.

Bonnie pulled out four tickets, which read 'Monty Lomax invites you to a special premiere of *Hound of the Baskervilles* at the Paramount Theatre in San Francisco!'

'Theo, you never cease to amaze me,' Cash exclaimed. 'How on earth –'

'They arrived the same morning as your letter,'

Theodore explained, 'but got overshadowed by the bad news from school.'

'What bad news?' Bonnie asked.

Theodore shrugged his shoulders. 'Bea and Carter got expelled,' he said, embarrassed.

Cash laughed out loud. It was not the reaction Theodore had been expecting.

'It's not funny!' he said. 'Three senior boys were seriously hurt!'

'Carter's been raised by Shadow Raptors all his life,' Cash pointed out, 'and you put him into a fancy school and then act surprised he got into a fight? That boy is definitely Franklin's son!'

Theodore sighed. 'It was Bea,' he admitted. 'She knocked two of them out cold and the other had a broken nose. She was protecting her brother.'

'Good for her,' Bonnie said, 'but with only four tickets we'll just have to make our apologies to our guests and suggest they do some sightseeing instead.'

'But if there are only four tickets,' Cash pointed out, 'how will you take all the children to the movies? You'll have to leave someone out. It really does make more sense for me to take Carter and Buster with me, Theodore.'

'Okay,' Theodore agreed reluctantly. 'And in the meantime, I have some business of my own to take care of,' he said somewhat cryptically. 'This is the perfect time to do it.'

✦ ✦ ✦

Early the next morning, Cash set off with a happy Carter riding atop Buster.

'Cash can fix anything, remember,' Bonnie said, tugging at Theodore's arm as he watched them ride off into the distance. 'He's also good at staying out of trouble,' she added.

Theodore turned and walked back up to the ranch. 'But Carter and Buster are excellent at getting *into* trouble, Bonnie,' he lamented. 'That's the issue.'

Anya and Lambert drove in at ten o'clock to find the three girls waiting on the porch with their bags.

Lambert greeted them in a jolly tone. 'Good morning, Kingsley girls. Going somewhere?'

'Aunt Bonnie is taking us to San Francisco!' Bea blurted out.

'And we're going to meet Monty Lomax!' gushed Violet.

Anya whistled as she wafted in. 'Are we? Well, that is a nice surprise. Some culture at last! How delightful – I can't wait!'

'But we only have four tickets,' Bea said.

'Where are we staying?' Anya asked, refusing to be put off, before walking purposefully into the house to find Bonnie.

'You can stay here, Mrs Kingsley. You won't have to worry about a thing,' Anya announced. 'I'll take very good care of them indeed.'

Bonnie was thrown off guard. 'Well, I was going –'

'Good, then that's settled,' Anya declared, as she inspected a silken glove, before Bonnie could collect her thoughts.

✦ ✦ ✦

Theodore was heading for the stables, a large pack on his back, when a shout from Lambert pulled him to a halt.

'I'm glad I caught you,' Lambert puffed. 'It looks like my wife has arranged with Mrs Kingsley to take Bea and her cousins to San Francisco for a few days.'

'Yes, all a bit last minute,' Theodore began to say, then something occurred to him. 'Hang on,' he said warily. 'Anya's taking them?'

'I think it's a wonderful idea,' Lambert said. 'Those girls need spoiling, and my wife will enjoy doing so – but where is Carter?'

'He wanted to see the countryside with his uncle, spend a bit of time together,' Theodore explained. 'He can't do cities – you should've seen him when we visited London.' Theodore smiled. 'But I thought San Francisco would be right up your street, Lambert?'

'Oh no,' the Viscount declared, 'shopping and premieres are my wife's pleasures, not mine. If I may make an observation – it looks as if you, too, are heading out on a journey?'

'Yes,' Theodore replied, 'I'm not a city person either, so I thought I'd have some time alone.'

'Let me ride with you, keep you company.'

'That's kind of you, Lambert,' Theodore said, deflecting him, 'but I'm happy alone, thanks.'

Lambert fixed him with a piercing stare. 'Let us put our cards on the table, Theodore. It's the journal,' Lambert said. 'You're looking for something connected with Franklin's journal. If so, I think I may be of some help.'

Theodore was stunned, both by Lambert's correct assumption and his forwardness.

'Yes, you're right,' replied Theodore politely, 'but I don't need any help. Now, if you don't mind, I have some things to get ready.'

'You're going to look for the twins,' Lambert said confidently.

Theodore turned round slowly. 'What makes you think that?'

Lambert gave an expansive gesture, and a smile. 'Theodore, my friend – why do you think I've come all the way from Europe to America?'

'You said you're inspecting a factory.'

Lambert nodded. 'Yes, my work is a good cover – and that's the reason my wife thinks we're here – but *you* must have wondered why I would come all this way.'

'Tell me,' Theodore said, intrigued.

'There was something I desperately wanted to discuss with you. This is where it all started for Franklin, so when I learnt you would be here it was essential I came.'

Theodore looked cautiously at him. 'What started here?'

'You and Franklin found the twins, just over twenty years ago, somewhere out here. I think I may be of some help in understanding what Franklin was researching, and how to find them once more. Perhaps a long ride is exactly what we both need to discuss this further – away from little ears.' He produced something from his pocket: a black pouch with a small round glistening stone. 'And I have this – a Saurman's keystone. My hope is it will help us find what we're looking for.'

13

The White Things

~ anything with claws and teeth ~

Buster happily trotted along, stopping every now and then to sniff the air. Cash looked at his riding partner in amazement. In spite of the fact that he had been raised by raptors and grown up outside of human influence, his long-lost nephew had adapted remarkably well to his new life, even if he seemed to prefer being alone. He'd picked up English very rapidly, but had no definite accent. When talking to Bea he spoke with an English one, but with him he spoke with an American one.

'Hey, Carter,' Cash said, 'tell me, can you make the sound of a tyrant?'

Carter turned round and let out the cold rattle Buster made to warn people away.

'Wow, that's great,' his uncle said, 'and the roar?'

Carter let out a series of load roars, causing Looper, Cash's allosaur, to glance at him in alarm.

'White Titan Tyrant has a different roar, like this,' Carter said, then perfectly imitated the sound, making Buster look at him quizzically.

'Ronax barks,' Carter offered, and again let loose a whole cacophony of noises one after another.

Of course, Cash had never heard any of these tyrants, but he was convinced the sounds were authentic, as they certainly spooked the saurs.

'Is that how you talk to the saurs?' he asked. 'Buster always knows what you want him to do.'

Carter smiled.

A mule deer bounded past, prompting Buster to go for it until it disappeared into the thicker bush.

'Coyotes, bobcats and foxes can be found around here as well,' Cash pointed out. 'Of course there were bigger carnivores at the top, before white folk came here. The Mountain Tyrants were the last to go; the only ones left are in a reserve way north of here. Before that, there were

several other tyrants and even Great Zinos with their elongated claws. There was balance. Then people came looking for gold and changed all that.'

'What are all the white things?' Carter asked, pointing to the many bleached objects scattered on the rocks.

'They're bones,' Cash replied sadly.

'Whose bones?'

'Apatos,' Cash replied. 'Lots of apatos.' He paused. 'They were killed for their tongues.'

Carter looked confused, so Cash stuck out his tongue. 'Tongues,' he said, pointing. 'When prospectors came out here they brought guns,' Cash elaborated. 'Anything with claws and teeth got the first bullets. These settlers brought dogs, and the rats followed. They like to eat saur eggs.'

Carter nodded, remembering his time on Aru.

'The people who didn't find any gold made their money selling apatos tongues. Apparently they're a delicacy.' Cash shook his head. 'Eventually this is what drove the native people away from here – the settlers made a claim on their land and the best way to get rid of them was to kill off the saurs they lived with. Around Lake Tahoe they took all the fish to move the Washoe people on, and on the plains they took away the bison and Brown Tyrants. All these wonderful animals were all deliberately wiped out in a matter of two or three years.'

'All gone?' Carter exclaimed, alarmed. 'But you have apatos.'

'Yes,' Cash explained, 'I keep a few and hope to reintroduce them to the area, bring back some of that balance.'

'The tritops and cattle are smaller and easier to keep,' Cash continued as they ambled along. 'Before refrigeration, meat spoiled quickly, so the livestock were taken by train to slaughterhouses. No train is big enough to take the apatos, so the tongues were cut from them and the rest was left to rot.'

Carter was silent for a while as it all sunk in, and then he spoke up. 'No raptors here?'

'There were, but this was a long time ago. Wherever humans populated the world the aggressive carnivores were always the first to be wiped out,' Cash said. 'Allosaurs, on the other hand, are different.' Cash patted Looper on the neck. 'They're not native to this area, and were the first saurs to be domesticated by humans. It's kept them from also being wiped out.'

It was clear the topic depressed Carter. There was another long pause as the boy made sense of what Cash was saying.

They continued to wander up further into the red hills, past the scattered white apatos bones and into the treeline, then Cash broke the silence. 'Tell me of Aru, your home.' He smiled at Carter.

Carter looked up. 'My clan, my family of Shadow Raptors?'

'Yes – your first family, the raptors – tell me about them.'

'No one wants me to talk of them,' Carter said ruefully. 'They think they killed my parents.'

'Do you miss them?'

'Yes,' Carter replied thoughtfully. 'They were hunted by stupid men. Not for tongues, but for feathers. Many saurs were hunted just for feathers.'

'Tell me, Carter, how did you talk to them?'

'Talk? No talking. Talking is what *you* do,' Carter explained. 'Saurs do not talk.'

'Okay then – how do they understand each other?'

Carter widened his eyes at Cash and gently lowered his head before flaring his nostrils. He let out a series of squawks and almost silent sharp inhalations of breath. 'Like that, except you can only see the face move. Not what is in my head.'

'So it's body movement and thought as well as saying something?' Cash queried.

'Not saying. Not talking. Not thinking. It's all feeling,' Carter elaborated.

'So how can you know what other raptors are saying?'

'You hear the sounds but it's not talking.' Carter tried to explain the difficult concept in a way that made sense. 'The sounds mean one thing, but the movements mean more. There is smell too, but I can't smell as well as Buster. This is only small part of it,' Carter added with a shrug.

'So another raptor comes up and moves a little, blinks and makes a strange noise – even farts – but that's only half of what it's communicating?'

Carter grinned. 'Yes, humans don't do it as well as saurs. I close my eyes but I still hear you make your sounds,' Carter ventured. 'I open my eyes and hide my ears, but see you move your hands, scrunch your face, and your lips make shapes. I close my eyes and hide my ears together, but still feel your message.'

'That's it, Carter,' Cash said warmly. 'Most humans only see and hear. We don't *feel* what is being said.'

Carter nodded. 'Bea can feel – she knows when I'm

sad, when I'm happy, when I'm hungry.'

'Yes,' Cash affirmed, 'that's called intuition. I guess we all have it but it's hard to explain.'

'Yes. Humans do it but not as well as saurs.'

'So that's how you communicate with Buster?'

'Yes,' Carter said.

'I know that also about Looper, my allosaur. But it took a long time with training for us to bond and for me to get to know his moods.'

'Yes – he likes you.'

'But other saurs – ones you have never met and are new to you – their sounds and movements are different and take time to learn?' Cash asked.

'Sure,' Carter replied with a grin. 'Just like learning to speak English.'

'But the feeling of kinship you have with the saurs is universal?' Cash pursued. 'It's the same for all saurs?'

'Yes,' Carter agreed, 'different but understandable. You know if Looper's hungry, if Violet and May are upset; you know if Bonnie wants a kiss. I am better than you at saurs because I'm half saur.'

The conversation was enlightening and to Cash everything seemed quite logical. Why wouldn't a boy in his unique circumstance have opened himself up to connect with, understand and communicate with the saurs around him? He nodded. 'I guess you are half saur.'

14

Hector's Exotic Pet Emporium

~ something extra special ~

Bea and her cousins sat in the very opulent lounge of the Grand Hotel in San Francisco with Anya Stitz, drinking tea and nibbling at the assortment of biscuits and small cakes displayed on the silver stand on their table. Or, rather, Violet and May did most of the munching. Anya – who rarely seemed to eat anything – sat and smiled indulgently at the girls as she sipped delicately from her cup.

'This stuff tastes weird!' Violet exclaimed after her first sip of tea. 'We only ever drink coffee at home.'

Bea felt sad that Bunty wasn't there with them. Bunty had always been fond of the finer things in life, and the tea made her miss her grandmother deeply. 'Have any of you ladies ever been to a premiere before?' asked Anya, breaking Bea out of her reverie. She surveyed them with a critical eye. 'We'll all need new dresses,' she said, 'so I suggest that's what we should do first – go shopping.'

Violet and May swung their legs and kicked each other under the table with excitement at the prospect of new clothes, but Bea spoke up.

'Thank you, Anya – this is all very kind of you, but I was hoping to wear the dress Monty gave me for my birthday,' she said.

Anya smiled broadly, but said airily and dismissively, 'Shopping for new things is what all young ladies should be doing.'

◆ ◆ ◆

After tea, Anya took them to a huge department store that boasted that it sold everything, making straight for the ladies' department on the second floor.

Right in front of the lift was a grand display of fashionable items. The girls all stood and gaped at the multitude of clothes and accessories.

'Remember, girls – get whatever you want,' said Anya, who already had whatever she wanted – except, that is, the girls eating out of her hand.

Bea, however, was standing there with a scowl on her face.

'What's the matter, Bea?' Anya asked.

'I've seen these feathers before,' she said slowly, 'but not like this, draped over a mannequin.'

'Would you like to try one on?' Anya asked, peering around. 'I can get an assistant to help us.'

'No thanks,' Bea said coldly.

'Good decision,' Anya said hurriedly. 'I used to wear feather boas all the time – could not *resist* buying them. I probably have hundreds back home in one of my wardrobes.'

'But they come from wonderful birds and raptors,' Bea pointed out.

'Yes, I used to think they were amazing too.' Anya sighed, a wistful look on her face.

Bea could see that Anya wasn't getting the message.

'The feathers *are* wonderful,' Bea tried to explain, 'but this feather boa is hideous!'

'I know,' trilled Anya. 'Fashion! One minute you're buying feather boas; the next, fur coats. I have a lot of those as well. Lamprecht always brings one back from a trip. I haven't worn most of them.'

It was no use – Bea's point was simply lost on Anya, who had turned away to stroke the soft leather of some gloves on display and called over an assistant, pointing at things she thought the girls would like, and then had them all boxed and bagged ready for her at the door.

On the way back to the hotel they stopped to look in the window of a shop in which four fluffy golden puppies bounced and rolled all over each other. Hector's Exotic Pet Emporium knew how to attract business, and always had children pressed up against its window cooing over the latest young arrivals.

The door swung open and out came a woman holding

a basket, followed by a young girl ecstatic with joy. 'Can I call it Mr Pop Sox, please, Mommy?' she pleaded.

'Girls, would *you* like a puppy each?' asked Anya.

All their mouths dropped at the same time. 'Seriously?'

'Why, yes, I love small pets. I have had many – they just melt my heart,' Anya replied.

'We already have a dog, two cats, four rabbits, two ducks and lots of chickens,' said May. 'Although I guess chickens and ducks don't count.'

'How many pets do you have?' asked Violet.

'None at the moment,' Anya conceded. 'I pass them on when they grow up. I prefer pets when they are like this, small and fluffy.'

'If you don't like these puppies, wait till you see what I have inside!' urged the shop assistant holding the door open and beckoning them in.

It seemed that Anya was determined to win them all over, and she thought Hector's Exotic Pet Emporium was going to be what got all three of them in one fell swoop.

◆ ◆ ◆

The front of the shop was devoted to kittens, rabbits and puppies, and other adorable furry creatures that the girls all wanted to stroke. Further back were smaller cages with glowing lamps heating up the reptiles. Lizards, spiders and snakes lazed around chewing grasshoppers and cockroaches. Barrel-sized cages swung overhead, containing exotic birds all squawking at each other, while a larger walk-in cage set against a side wall housed a multitude of smaller birds all singing for their freedom.

The further into the shop they ventured, the less any of them wanted a new pet. The twins started talking about the pets they already loved, and Bea reasoned that whatever it was that she got she'd have to look after that as well as Theodore and Carter . . . in addition to Buster, who now had to wear a chain round his neck.

But Anya was clearly not going to be put off that easily.

'We're looking for something extra special,' she told the assistant. 'Something totally unusual . . . something exotic perhaps?'

The man beamed. 'We're not called Hector's Exotic Pet Emporium for nothing, ma'am. You may be in luck. One of our overseas dealers, whom we don't often see, came by this very morning with something quite unusual.'

'Sounds interesting,' Anya said. 'Girls, what do you think?'

Bea was off the pet idea completely now, but was curious to know what the man had, so she nodded.

'Now, we don't usually sell these,' the man continued. 'It's quite a rare thing to see in this country, or even the country it comes from, so I'm told. Honestly, I don't know any other person who's got one.'

'What is it?' Anya demanded.

The man turned and walked through a curtain across a wide doorway and was gone for a little while before he walked back in holding a large cage. All four of them looked on with wide eyes. The creature was turned away from them, cowering in the back of the cage, a bright bundle of colourful feathers roughly the size of a fox.

'Not sure exactly what type it is, but it's come all the way from someplace in Indonesia, I think,' the man told them as they strained to see it.

Its head turned and extended out to look at them, then it rolled over onto its belly, kicked out two bright yellow legs from its mass of feathers, and stood up with a good shake and a flap. A long black tail with peculiar-shaped feathers along the side whipped out from behind. It twitched its head from side to side, blinked at them with its bright pink eyes, and let out a little squawk.

Bea gasped. 'It's a Raptor of Paradise!'

15

The Old Dead Tree

~ the cavernous terrain below ~

T he sun beat down on Theodore and Lambert as they moved slowly across the desert. They were heading south, towards the flatter, more open territory of the Sacramento Basin.

Theodore scanned the horizon, searching for the signs that would tell him he was close. He looked across at Lambert, and said in a casual tone, 'Back at Bunty's lodge in Kenya, you said that Franklin mentioned me and the twins.'

'You have a good memory,' said Lambert, smiling. 'Yes, that's right.'

'Well, it doesn't,' said Theodore. 'In fact, the journal you gave me has several pages missing. Did you take them?'

'Certainly not!' cried Lambert. 'Why would I? Perhaps Franklin tore the pages out himself.'

'It wouldn't have been like him to do that,' said Theodore thoughtfully. 'No other journal of his has pages missing. So how did you come to know about Frank and me finding the twins?'

'He mentioned it within the first ten minutes of our meeting,' Lambert said. 'And your name kept popping up for the next week we were in Aru. How could I forget it? However, at the time, his long conversations regarding Saurmen and keystones seemed . . . well, it all seemed quite far-fetched. He insisted there was a temple on the island and he was going to find it without a map. All the locals thought he was mad, including me. Anyhow, it was about a year or so after I got back home and fully recovered from my horrendous ordeal that I picked up Franklin's journal and started to read it. And here's the funny thing: if I had never met the man, I would have said they were the writings of a complete lunatic, or the plot of a fanciful children's story.'

'Yes, it does read like that to some degree,' agreed Theodore.

'But he wasn't crazy,' Lambert went on. 'So I showed his journal to a few learned friends of mine.'

'Friends?'

'Academic types,' said Lambert. 'All well read and up on history, and so on. All but one thought it was a load of silly nursery rhymes, nonsense, the wild imagination of a deluded man.'

'And?' Theodore prodded.

Lambert smiled. 'Well, his eye lit up and he took a great interest in what I was telling him. He told me what he knew of keystones and the Saurman Empire. It wasn't a lot – I don't think anyone knows that much. It's mostly hearsay and legend, but paired with what Franklin had in his journal it added flesh to the bones of the myth and became . . . real. I began my own research, and thanks to my shipping company was able to travel and follow up leads.'

'What did you find?' asked Theodore, intently curious.

'Probably the same as Franklin,' Lambert admitted. 'Fragments of stories, a prophecy about a child – half man half saur – who will bring order to the world. Even rumours of a lost city somewhere in what is now Mexico, and temples dotted around the world. Sadly I've found no temples or treasure. But there must be something in all this nevertheless. There seem to be generations of people protecting something – a secret order – hiding the truth for someone special to come along and –'

'I have to stop you, Lambert,' Theodore interrupted. 'The Saurman Empire is nothing but dust.'

'There are the keystones,' Lambert reminded him. 'It is said that all Saurmen have keystones, and, as we both know, occasionally these strange opalised dinosaur bones pop up around the world.'

'So where did you get yours?' Theodore asked.

'Christie's auction house,' said Lambert matter-of-factly. 'It was part of the estate of an eccentric collector, but I knew instantly it was not an ethnic ornamental charm. I guess that owning it now makes me a Saurman.'

'Not exactly,' said Theodore. 'According to Franklin's earlier journal, you have to be given one by another Saurman.'

Lambert shrugged. 'Perhaps that's why I haven't had much luck with mine.'

'And the twins, how do you know about the twins?' asked Theodore.

'The day I met your dear friend he said something that stuck with me. He said that all this started when you and he found two very dead twins, and he took a keystone from one of them. He showed it to me. It looked magical. Anyway, he said that if he hadn't taken it, he probably wouldn't have had a baby son on the other side of the world away from home, and we wouldn't be celebrating in a bar on a remote island.'

'And, to further that point,' Theodore added, 'you and I wouldn't be riding out into the Californian desert discussing this some twelve years later.'

'Exactly. Franklin said it was destiny that our paths had crossed.'

Theodore nodded. 'Perhaps.'

'Our chance meeting through Carter; him saving me at that polo game in Africa, of all places – it's no surprise. It was our destiny, Theodore.'

'Thank goodness no one is around to hear this mumbo-jumbo conversation,' muttered Theodore uncomfortably. 'They'd think we were mad.'

His words had no effect on Lambert, who was enlarging enthusiastically on his theme. 'I now believe we're here to finish what Franklin started: find the missing pieces and solve the puzzle – and Carter has something to do with it!'

◆ ◆ ◆

Later that day, the Viscount wiped the sweat from his face with his handkerchief, and glanced at Theodore, who sat astride his allosaur looking out at the vast desert.

'Theodore, forgive me for questioning you again, but do you know where we are going?'

Theodore continued to stare out at the landscape. Eventually he answered.

'Not exactly. But I'll know when we find it.' He urged his allosaur onwards and rode on into the baking sand. Lambert followed.

A while later, Lambert pressed his companion again.

'Tell me – how did you and Franklin first find the twins?' he asked.

'We were in a sandstorm and had no shelter or cover,' said Theodore. 'The land was flat as far as you could see. Anyway, the storm whipped up around us and we couldn't ride our allos safely, so we trudged on, leading them by foot. Then out of nowhere, there was an old dead tree – almost out of the blue – right in front of us. And that's where they were.'

'So we're looking for a dead tree?'

'Yep,' said Theodore with a nod.

'I wonder if it was a temple tree you found,' Lambert mused. 'There's a page in the journal about sacred temple trees that grew atop the old stone temples buried under them.'

Theodore smiled. 'Under them, you say? Wait until you see what's under this tree.'

'*These old stone structures crumbled,*' Lambert continued, '*and nature took them back to the earth from where they came. From it a new temple grew in the form of a tree, I think the passage reads.*' Lambert paused. 'We're talking about thousands of years ago, remember, so your very dead tree would fit the story. Anyhow – shouldn't you have to have a keystone and be a true Saurman to find a temple?'

'That keystone of yours, Lambert,' Theodore mused, 'have you ever had it work in some strange way . . . felt some power from it, or had a strange moment where it connected with you?'

'Never,' admitted Lambert ruefully. 'But, as you said, it could be because I'm not its rightful owner.' He peered up at the sun blazing down on them. 'It's a pity – it's getting really hot out here, and I could do with the shade of a tree – or anything, for that matter. But there's nothing here. Just sand and rocks as far as the eye can see.'

Suddenly Theodore stopped and pointed. 'There!' he said. 'That tree! Let's walk from here,' Theodore suggested. 'Close your eyes and let your allosaur lead you; trust it and take it one step at a time.'

'You're tricking me, Theodore!' Lambert protested.

'I'm not,' he insisted. 'Trust the saur.'

They continued silently for a few minutes, before Theodore asked the Viscount to open his eyes. Lambert

blinked them
open to let in the
blinding sunlight,
and standing
just before him
was the gnarled
and twisted
remains of a
very old tree.

'My goodness, I thought you were pulling my leg!' he exclaimed in shock.

Still adjusting to the light, Lambert walked towards the tree.

'Stop!' shouted Theodore – but it was too late.

The old dead tree was hanging perilously on the edge of a rocky outcrop, with a huge canyon split into the ground below it. Not realising this, Lambert stumbled, rolling over to one side and down a long narrow pathway leading from the tree down into the cavernous terrain below.

16

The Bear and the Wolf

~ *people etched onto the rock face* ~

The elevations up in the Red Hills were marked by the different fauna that grew there, and Carter noticed the changes as he and Cash crept up into pine-filled forests. They passed several dried-up ponds and waterways where yellow-legged frogs and turtles tussled for the last moist patches drying up in the heat of the day.

'It's not just people who are suffering from the drought – everything is perishing out here,' Cash observed.

In the late afternoon they came to a sheltered clearing and decided to rest the saurs and eat. Carter stretched his legs and found a strange wooden structure overgrown with weeds and falling apart from years of neglect. It ran from the rock face, and on closer inspection proved to be an old boarded-up mineshaft complete with a stack of twisted, rusting metal posts and an old cart dumped outside.

'There are hundreds of these old mines dotted about,' Cash told his nephew. 'Long ago, water was used to dislodge rock and move the sediment – the grit and mud – down these wooden sluices.'

'Where is the water now?' Carter was quick to ask.

'That's exactly what we're here to find out, my boy,' Cash said. 'When this place was up and running, the water was redirected from springs into an ever-narrowing channel, through a large canvas hose, and out through a giant iron nozzle. Anyhow, the high-pressure stream was used to wash entire hillsides through these sluices, and many people sifted through them to find the gold. Eventually hydraulic mining was stopped because of the vast areas of land down there –' Cash pointed to where they had come from – 'in the Sacramento Valley, which were devastated by flood waters and the sediment choking up the farmland.'

Carter stood on tiptoes to try to see where his uncle was pointing.

'The other areas, where the water once ran, became a dust bowl. But springs don't just run dry. The missing water must be *somewhere* – I'm hoping we're going to find where the water's being diverted.'

They gathered themselves and were about to head off when Buster got a sniff of something. His nostrils flared widely and he looked about, searching for whatever it was. Carter smoothed some of the tyrant's jet-black feathers to settle him but Buster twitched, lowered his head and let out a low and unsettling rattle. At that moment a huge brown bear – some ten feet tall – reared out of the treeline and took a swipe at Cash and Looper. This sudden movement sent the skittish allosaur up and into a spin.

'Whoa!' Cash cried, full of alarm. 'Watch out, Carter!'

Suddenly a strange man appeared from behind them waving his arms while stepping cautiously forward. He wore a poncho of animal furs with a collar made from an assortment of feathers. The mighty bear grunted, then settled back down on all fours with a mighty thud. The man continued waving away the bear and the bear promptly obliged.

Cash was astonished. Carter was more fixated on the strange man who lowered his arms and shrugged at them both.

'You two all right?' the man called.

Cash dismounted, patting Looper on the neck to settle him down, while Carter slid off Buster's back.

'Yes, thank you,' said a stunned Cash.

The man was clearly a Native American, with a face full of worldly experience and long black hair that hung in a plait down his back. 'What tyrant is that?' the man asked.

'A Black Dwarf Tyrant – he's called Buster,' Carter replied.

The stranger walked over and patted the tyrant on the flank, then walked round and under his tail in awe. Buster was still unsettled and kept one of his caustic yellow eyes on the man throughout. Unlike the men at the county fair, he seemed to be at ease with Buster, confident and interested. 'Never seen an all-black one,' the man commented, and as he came round to the front he gently lifted his hand and pulled Buster's jaw open to have a look inside by holding on to one of his large front teeth. Carter and Cash didn't know what to make of it.

'Lips, gums and tongue – black also,' the man said.

He let go of the front tooth, but Buster remained open-mouthed and stared with amazement at the man who was now parting the feathers around his face. 'Skin black too, very strange.'

He patted the feathers back into place and looked around to the tyrant's forearms, and the elongated flap of skin adjoining the body that had an unusual amount of densely packed feathers. 'Good for swimming.'

The man dipped his hand into this mass and rummaged around before yanking a feather out. Buster was too stunned at the sudden inspection to react.

The man sniffed the feather and ran it between his fingers before walking on and taking another longer feather from Buster's back hip. This made Buster flinch, but the man patted him gently. 'Thank you, friend,' he said, then sniffed and felt the second feather before comparing them side by side. 'Tyrant eat fish but not lately,' the man noted. 'He needs oils.'

The man stuffed the feathers into a pocket and then Carter noticed more keenly the collar of feathers he wore. 'I used to have one of those,' he said.

'Good for keeping rain off poncho,' the man confirmed.

'What tribe you from?'

'Shadow Raptors,' Carter said with pride.

The man shook his head. 'Never heard of them; they East Coast?'

'They're from Aru in Indonesia, the other side of the

world from here, and so is the tyrant,' Cash explained.

'You lost?' the man asked.

'No – I'm from down there.' Cash pointed back to the landscape that spread out down below the treeline.

'I'm Wolf from the Washoe,' the man said.

'I'm Carter, and he is Uncle Cash,' Carter offered. 'What was that?'

'Grizzly bear, male, hungry. You never seen bear before?' the man said.

Carter shook his head.

The man smiled. 'I've never seen Black Tyrant before.'

'How did you manage to scare the bear away?' asked Cash.

The man shrugged his shoulders, and said, 'I told him you were not tasty. Make his tummy ill.'

'You can talk to bears?'

The man nodded. 'Sure, like you can talk to saurs.'

Cash and Carter exchanged a glance. The whole situation was mind-boggling. Had he been following and overhearing their conversation?

'Where are you heading, Mr Wolf?' asked Cash.

'Nowhere, anywhere, everywhere – and it's just Wolf, named after my parents,' he replied.

Cash opted for a new topic of conversation. 'We're looking for the source of the water that runs down from here,' he explained. 'Our wells have run dry and now some of the springs run with red water.'

Wolf thought. 'That is not good. Without water nothing survives. Everything has to drink, including the trees.'

'Have you seen where the water might be going?'

'Mmm, not sure where the water is going.' He rubbed his chin. 'But I have seen where there is red water, a few hours ride from here – I will show you.'

The man darted up a slope and came back minutes later leading a magnificent pale grey horse. He pointed to Buster and said softly to the horse, 'Told you so, jet black all over,' before mounting it and riding on ahead. Carter and Buster followed. Cash tugged on his reins to follow two of the most interesting people he had ever met further into the Red Hills.

♦ ♦ ♦

The riding was easy as they followed the old mining routes that weaved round the low mountain range, created by years of hard work cutting back and levelling the otherwise treacherous land. Carter and Wolf, who seemed to get along very well, both understood each other's odd way with animals and interest in all living things. Cash rode behind, observing and learning, but it was now getting dark and he could feel the chill higher up in the hills. He shuddered, trying not to think about what could be mutilating the saurs, or about the size of the bears around these parts.

Wolf dismounted from his horse. 'We must rest

here tonight and visit the red water in the morning,' he announced. Cash looked about. In all his years in this part of the world he'd never been to this place. It was like someone had cut a perfectly deep pathway through the red rocks with a clear view of the mountain range in front.

'Those miners certainly worked hard for a living,' Cash commented as he got off Looper and let him go free to find something for dinner.

'This place existed long before gold miners came,' said Wolf.

Cash looked about as he gathered firewood. 'I beg to differ,' he said, 'the walls here are perfectly vertical.' He patted one, and a heavy red mineral dust lifted off it. 'This was surely cut within the last hundred years.'

Carter pointed something out on the smooth rock face further along. 'Look – people!' he exclaimed.

Cash swung his head round, expecting to see someone approaching, but realised Carter was pointing to a group of crude drawings of people etched onto the rock face.

They went closer to examine it. The figures were only about a hand high and set about half an inch into the rock. They were marked with what could be charcoal or soot. The figures were not those from a child's drawings; they were bold and confident, but simple in form. Around the figures were a host of mammals, birds and saurs. The deer, cows and tritops could be made out easily with their different and distinctive horns. Smaller goats with curled horns were harder to recognise, and the smaller four-legged creature was either a wolf, dog or big cat. Perhaps they were domesticated, being close to the humans. Further away from the centre were the bigger and unmistakable creatures like the apatos, bison, zinos and tyrants.

'Why would miners make art on the walls like this?' Cash asked Wolf.

'These were here long before the white man came, and way before my people,' he answered.

'They're so well preserved!' Cash exclaimed.

Wolf nodded. 'Long before us, Saurmen lived here.'

♦ ♦ ♦

The evening passed and Cash and Wolf were out like candles, but Carter remained awake, gazing up at the multitude of stars high above him. He sat up and looked around. The last embers of the flickering fire made the ancient people and creatures appear to dance on the walls. Carter quietly stepped away from the warmth of Buster's feathers and walked a little further away up the open path.

That's when he heard the cry.

The sound carried no anger or aggression, and probably sounded louder than it was because in the silence it echoed around him. The strange cry rang out again.

It was a piercing cry – something was in distress and calling out. Carter had no idea what it was, as everything on this continent was new to him, but he felt it was somehow calling out for him.

17

The Premiere

~ *this mystery celebrity* ~

'Monty Lomax!' gushed Violet. 'I've seen all his movies!'

'And Micki Myers is incredible!' May said.

There was no mistaking that the part of the trip everyone was looking forward to was the premiere and meeting its star, Monty Lomax. Even Anya had questions for Bea about the Hollywood heart-throb. 'He is such a handsome man,' she sighed.

Bea had as much to say for her real hero, Micki Myers, who preferred to be behind the camera and out of the limelight. She described Micki's most recent assignment, recording the tribes who lived along the mighty Amazon River, many of whom had never seen a white woman before, let alone one armed only with a camera.

'Mom gets the magazines with Micki's photos in. She does sensational stuff!' May and Violet confirmed.

Anya was less easily impressed, however, and recoiled at Micki's habit of wearing a man's flying suit and travelling to places where there was no electricity.

Bea found herself getting nervous about the possibility of meeting her old friends again. 'I haven't seen them since the funeral, so perhaps they won't remember me,' she said humbly.

'Wait till they hear you've come all the way from England to the premiere!' shouted May.

'No!' exclaimed Bea, alarmed.

The two girls looked astonished.

'I don't want to interfere – they have important people to meet,' said Bea. 'It wouldn't be right.'

'Of course they want to meet up with you!' burst out Violet. 'Are you nuts? This is Monty Lomax and Micki Myers, for heaven's sakes! Please don't be shy all of a sudden – we all want to meet them!'

'Yes!' May chimed in. 'They'll be so upset if we don't say hello! They sent Theodore the tickets specially.'

'No!' insisted Bea, and the firmness of her tone took both girls aback. 'Promise me you won't say anything to them. Or to any of their people.'

Violet and May looked at one another, helpless and unhappy.

'But . . .' began May.

'Promise!' Bea demanded.

The two girls looked at one another and sighed heavily.

'Okay,' said a deflated Violet. 'We promise we won't say anything about you being here.'

'Thank you,' said Bea.

◆ ◆ ◆

The chauffeur-driven car pulled up to the red carpet, where a man in a top hat opened the door and bowed. Anya, who was well accustomed to this sort of reception, played it cool. She walked to the centre of the carpet and posed for pictures wearing her most elegant dress and expression.

This put her some distance away from Bea and the twins, who nervously grinned and waved. The twins wore their new clothes, and Bea wore the short fashionable dress that Monty had given her on her birthday, while clutching the camera from Micki as if it was a handbag.

Once inside, they milled around trying to spot famous faces, of which there were many, and when a gong chimed Bea took her seat along with Anya, Violet and May. The lights in the theatre went down, and a master of ceremonies strode out onto the stage towards a microphone.

'Good evening, ladies and gentlemen!' he barked. 'And welcome to the Paramount Theatre for this wonderful premiere of *The Hound of the Baskervilles*, starring the fantastic Monty Lomax!'

At his name, the whole crowd erupted into cheers and ecstatic applause, Bea, Violet and May joining in enthusiastically. Anya, meanwhile, retained her usual aloof expression.

'And here, to introduce the movie, please welcome

none other than Monty Lomax himself, accompanied by his great friend the world-famous photographer Micki Myers!'

As Monty and Micki appeared from the side of the stage, Bea found herself rising to her feet, along with the rest of the audience, clapping her hands. Only Anya remained seated, her one concession to the wild applause

being a delicate wave of her hand towards the stage.

Monty looked as handsome as ever, and Micki just as beautiful.

'Thank you so much for that wonderful reception,' said Monty when the applause finally died down and the audience had retaken their seats. 'It is such a pleasure to be here with you today to share this film with you. And it is especially auspicious because someone very important

to both of us is in the audience this evening – someone who had a major impact on us when we met her in Kenya last year.'

Micki stepped forward to the microphone and said, 'This person is one of the bravest people Monty and I have ever known. She thinks of herself as just an ordinary girl –'

'But she is far from ordinary!' said Monty, beaming. 'Bea Kingsley, we know you're here!' he called out, searching the crowd with his eyes. 'Come and join us!'

'You said you wouldn't tell them!' Bea hissed at her cousins, mortified. 'You promised!'

'We promised not to *say* anything to them,' said May.

'So we didn't,' grinned Violet. 'We wrote them a note and passed it to someone instead.'

Immediately the audience began to turn their heads to spot this mystery celebrity. When Bea showed no sign of getting to her feet, Violet took control.

'She's here!' she shouted, standing up and waving.

May grabbed Bea by the arm and forced her to her feet. 'Here she is!' she yelled.

The audience erupted, whistling and cheering and stamping and clapping, as Violet and May gripped their cousin's arms firmly and pushed her into the aisle, and then towards the stage.

Bea felt as if she was in a dream. As soon as Monty and Micki embraced her she felt her anxiety recede, along with much of the tension that had built up, without her really

knowing it, ever since losing Bunty in Kenya. For the first time in a very long time she didn't feel so alone.

Monty and Micki generously explained how they had met Bea, and dedicated the film to her dearly missed grandmother. Bea, relieved that her beloved Bunty was the main focus of their attention, was asked to say something, but only managed to note that she wished her brother Carter was here to join them.

The film was a huge success, and to Bea's surprise Monty's British accent had improved greatly. There was even a part in the film where Doctor Watson said a few remarks that reminded her of Theodore. In that moment she regretted that he wasn't here to share the experience, and she wished she hadn't been so hard on him.

After the credits rolled, Bea, her cousins and Anya were escorted backstage to meet up with Monty and Micki.

The twins almost fainted at the thrill of being hugged by the man whose face was plastered all over town on posters, and who'd appeared on the big screen moments earlier. Micki was just as eager to meet more Kingsley girls, who immediately set about trying to impress with tales of their antics at the county fair.

Micki did not warm to Anya that well, but Monty charmed her, and they had a brief chat about her husband Lambert, of whom Monty was very fond.

'So where are Carter and Theo?' asked Monty.

Bea did her best to pass on fond greetings and feeble excuses, but Monty could see something was up.

'Is everything all right, Bea?' Monty asked a bit more privately, away from Anya and her cousins, who'd pressed Micki into showing them her latest photos.

'To be honest, no,' Bea admitted. 'I'm worried about Buster, his having to be chained up is just the tip of the iceberg. Theo tries, but –' she raised her eyes – 'and as for Carter, I think he's still finding it hard to fit in – you know, being human.'

'Okay, leave this with me,' Monty announced. 'Tell me, does your uncle have a runway on his ranch? No? Too bad – but I know Theodore is very good at clearing one.' Monty winked at Bea, who felt better now that she'd confided in him. 'Make sure he preps one,' he told her.

'When did you arrive?' Micki quizzed the girls. 'Have you been exploring San Francisco? This place is buzzing!'

'We found a Raptor of Paradise,' said Violet.

'In a pet store,' added May.

'Really?' said Micki, astonished. 'Is that legal?'

'It's not,' interrupted Bea. 'The assistant told us himself.'

'So did you buy it?' Micki asked.

'No,' said Bea regretfully.

'Good,' said Micki. 'You'd just be creating a market for these crooked pet shops to sell more. Buying one would put you on the wrong side of the law and at the end of a long chain of illegal black market trafficking.'

The girls all looked at one another a bit sheepishly, and Anya turned a shade paler than she usually was.

'Actually the shop assistant refused to sell it to us,' Bea owned up.

'I don't understand,' said Micki.

'I wanted to buy it,' Anya chipped in. 'I even offered double whatever he wanted for it,' she said. 'But he wouldn't be moved.'

'I thought perhaps if we'd bought it we could save it – I don't know – to let it loose so it could be free,' Bea reasoned. 'Carter could tell us what type it was.'

Micki smiled at Bea. 'I totally understand why you would want to buy it. You have the biggest heart of all, Bea, and freeing it would of course be your priority. But why would the evil pet store owner not sell it to you? It's his business and makes no sense.'

'We only spoke to the sales assistant,' said Bea, adding that he had actually seemed a very kind man.

'And by all accounts, Hector, his boss, sounded like a decent man as well,' Violet added. 'He only bought the raptor because the trader was treating it badly.'

'Oh, I see,' Micki said and reclined into her chair silently.

Monty turned to Micki. 'You have that look again,' he said.

Bea, Violet, May and Anya all turned to Micki.

'What look?' Micki said innocently.

'She's making a cunning plan – I've seen it before when an assignment or idea pops into her head,' Monty said proudly.

Micki rocked forward, and they all huddled in to hear what she had to say.

'Anya,' she said, fixing her with a penetrating look, 'I don't know you very well, but have you ever thought of doing any acting?'

Anya was surprised at the question, and that it was directed to her.

'Why, yes,' she answered, 'I have always wanted a starring role in something. What do you have in mind?'

'A rich, aristocratic European woman who simply *must* have a Raptor of Paradise to please her "daughter".' Micki grinned, and with a sweep of her arm indicated Bea.

18

The Twins

~ *two halves of the same thing* ~

'There are a lot of skeletons down here,' Lambert called up.

'Yep,' Theodore agreed from above the canyon.

'All fallen into this trap, no doubt,' Lambert continued to himself.

'I think you will find that you're the only one who's fallen in,' Theodore mumbled under his breath.

Theodore tied their allosaurs to the tree, looped the end of a large coil of rope to the trunk, and tossed it down into the ravine. The end slapped a rock close to Lambert and startled him. 'Steady on,' he uttered.

'Sorry,' Theodore called as he made his way down the rope, rather than taking the long way round.

'Easy mistake, falling in here,' Lambert said, as Theodore approached. 'Looks like it's also snared many saurs over the years. They can't have seen the ravine below, then fallen in and died a slow death. Reminds me of the La Brea Tar Pits in California – you familiar with them, Theodore?'

Theodore nodded.

'That dead tree up there is what's luring creatures to their death down here,' Lambert surmised. 'This is no temple; it's a death trap.'

Theodore shrugged and kept his thoughts to himself.

The scale of the canyon was deceptive. The sides shot upwards steeply, and ended dramatically with the blue sky above. The canyon's chill was refreshing at first, and their sweaty backs prickled. The complete silence highlighted every stone that cracked underfoot and the stillness of breeze was haunting. They slowly made their way through the canyon, but as it was slightly curved, they couldn't see where it was leading. 'It's hard to make out the size of this place,' Lambert said softly, and the words reverberated around them, the stone walls bouncing what little vibration there was and amplifying it.

Theodore let Lambert take it in and decided not to fill in any details. Theodore knew that soon enough he'd map what was around him in his mind and realise how unique the place was.

Theodore leant against a wall and watched Lambert move round the skeletons that filled the canyon's basin. He could see that Lambert was looking too much at the detail and not at the bigger picture. He lifted some large apatos ribs out of the way to get around, and tossed a few other bones aside with his foot.

Theodore, seeing Lambert was looking for human

bones amongst the millions of saur bones like needles in this calcified haystack, couldn't contain himself any longer.

'Haven't you noticed, Lambert, the way all the skeletons are laid out?' he asked.

Lambert looked up and pondered. 'No,' he replied. 'It's just a mess of mixed-up bones.'

'You sure of that?' Theodore climbed up a few rocks and looked down. 'Try getting a better view.'

As Lambert scrambled clumsily to a higher vantage point at the other side of the canyon, Theodore started to explain what he knew. 'These bones, they all look like they've laid down to rest – not fallen down into the canyon, like you did. None have been scavenged and scattered by hungry saurs, or trampled on in a desperate bid to get out.' Lambert looked around at the sight below him as Theodore continued. 'What's stranger is that they all point the same way – look: all the skulls are on this side.'

'My goodness – you're right!' Lambert exclaimed. 'How did I miss that?'

'You're too concerned about finding the twins amongst all this,' Theodore suggested. 'When Frank and I found this canyon, it took us a while before we realised what this place is.'

Lambert looked around, still trying to gather his thoughts. 'Go ahead and tell me, Theodore,' he said hopelessly. 'Please don't let me guess and embarrass myself.'

Theodore fingered the band of his hat, which he held

in his hand. 'It's a mass saur graveyard,' he said. 'These creatures all came here on purpose to die in this place.' He pointed over to the far end, to where they had not yet ventured. 'By the tree it's not as deep, so they make their way carefully down the slope either side. They all head that way.' Theodore showed Lambert where the canyon went deeper and curved round a bend. 'Notice how they all lay down only pointing that way.'

Lambert's jaw dropped. 'My word, you're right! But how would they know to come here, and why?'

Theodore smiled at Lambert, who was now asking the right questions and getting the bigger picture.

Lambert pointed towards the end of the canyon. 'I'm taking a calculated guess that the only human bones are the twins, and they're at the end where all the saurs are facing?' he offered hopefully.

Theodore nodded. 'Let's go and pay them a visit.'

Lambert smiled. He was glad Theodore had let him at least get to the point of it all rather than scrabble about for days trying to find them. Like Theodore had pointed out, if you kept close to the walls of the canyon it was easier to traverse the multitude of bones. Lambert made another well-informed guess. 'It's getting denser here closer to the end of the canyon,' he mused, 'as if the saurs all tried one by one to get that bit closer, drawn in like magnets. And these are probably the oldest of all the skeletons, the most recent being at the back, way over there.' Lambert waved behind him as Theodore nodded.

'That was our guess as well,' he confirmed.

As the canyon walls grew closer and higher, Lambert grew more curious – but then something changed about the rock face at the end of the canyon where they were heading. Carved into the side there looked to be the front of a building. It had several pillars about three storeys high and a central section that appeared to have an open doorway set into it.

Theodore took his time; after all, he'd been here before. Lambert, however, grew overexcited and made his way quickly up to the front of it.

It seemed to be just a facade of a building, and around it crude pictures of people and saurs of all descriptions were etched into the walls and columns. The central doorway was several feet deep with soot-blackened walls, but was very narrow; there was only room for one person to inch in at a time. The saur skeletons right at the front were piled very high and seemed like they were frozen into a permanent pose looking towards the doorway. Lambert eagerly clambered over them, tossing the odd bone aside to ease his passage.

And there, just inside, at the back of the deep doorway, were two human skeletons slumped together.

Lambert had to pull away the last few saur skeletons to get a better view and illuminate the scene. Theodore made his way in and stood back in the shadows, holding the palm of his hand over the hilt of the knife sheathed to his belt. The metal was cold, but the stone was almost uncomfortably hot.

Lambert knelt down in front of the twin skeletons that all the saur skeletons were facing, and stared at them both. The two human skeletons were sitting nearly upright, leaning in and propping one another up. Both were swathed in a thin and fragile material, and their arms were wrapped round each other, perhaps in an embrace.

'Why would you think they're twins?' Lambert questioned. The air was so still that the mere exhalation of air from his mouth seemed to lift a light layer of soot and dust off the walls. 'To me they look more like lovers, embraced for eternity.'

Theodore waited for the air to settle and replied. 'They're twins all right, not lovers.'

'How do you know that?' said Lambert.

Theodore smiled to himself but was silent.

'Theodore, look – they're holding each other – see how they have been bound together. Probably husband and wife. Perhaps even a king and queen – they're so old they could even be Adam and Eve!' Lambert grinned at his own joke and carried on. 'These two were probably revered or worshipped, and in death bound together for the afterlife, probably by devoted followers. You know, all the great explorers have discovered things like this. Surely Franklin would have known this as well? He admired Howard

Carter a great deal – even named his son after him! The Valley of the Kings, the Queen's Chamber . . . It's obvious they're not twins, but some long-forgotten royalty.'

Theodore hung back and remained silent, which annoyed Lambert.

'The keystones, two halves of a single bone,' Lambert continued. 'I wonder which twin has the remaining one?'

'The one on the left,' Theodore called to him. 'Be careful with the fabric that binds them,' he warned, 'it's fragile, and we don't want to desecrate this grave any more than we have already. While you're there,' he added, 'take a look below.'

Lambert considered his words and gently edged closer to the two skeletons. They had slumped forward over the years and the fabric that wrapped round them seemed to be the only thing holding them up. It ended where the knees would have been, but the leg bones had fallen to the side a little. The air was so still and cold that Lambert could hear his own heartbeat as he lightly lifted the fine fabric away from over the right skeleton's shoulder. The very end gave way and turned to dust, but there was enough substance in the rest of it to lift up from the ribcage and away from the skeleton leaning in on the left.

And there it was: the other half of the Saurman keystone. It was just like the one Franklin had showed him all those years ago that had caught his attention and so bewitched him. It was an object he knew so well – and here was its opposite, the other part of a perfectly formed small dinosaur bone that had somehow been opalised over the course of 200 million years, and found its way from Australia to North America, and then come to be round the neck of a skeleton in a saur graveyard. Even here, in the dimness of a shallow doorway in the side of a deep canyon, it managed to catch a slither of light and burst back into life.

Lambert sighed with ecstasy. 'It's beautiful.'

When Lambert let the fabric go it fell into pieces, and then into dust that wafted away in the stirred-up air. He reached out and took the stone in his hand, lifting it away from the ribcage a little, before realising he would have to get the pendant over the skull. This looked tricky – but it was already in his hand; it was already his. So he jerked it, quickly severing the skull from the neck bones in an instant, the way a magician removes a cloth from a table without disturbing any of the glasses or cutlery. The skull fell forward but Lambert immediately caught it in his other hand and resettled it at a new angle atop the cradle of bones.

The keystone set in Theodore's knife suddenly went cold. 'You okay in there?' he called out.

Lambert finally exhaled as he palmed the pendant. It was free from where it had been hidden away for hundreds, even thousands, of years – and now it was his. 'All fine, thanks, just taking a good look,' he replied, then thrust the keystone into his pocket.

'Good,' Theodore called out. 'I need to get the keystone – it's not safe in there any more.'

Theodore would come in and find it gone, so Lambert had to think fast. 'Let me get it for you . . .' he mumbled, quickly taking the pendant back out of his pocket and pretending he was gently removing it from the skeleton the way he should have done beforehand. Theodore could only see the back of him from where he was standing. 'Got it!' he said.

'Can you see why they're twins and not lovers?' Theodore asked.

Lambert pulled his gaze away from the keystone glistening in his hand and looked down to where the fabric had pulled away from round the waist to see something unusual. The pelvis was wider than normal, and misshapen. He peered closer. Into the hips fed two spines, where the skeletons were fused together. They were conjoined twins. Two halves of the same thing, both one and two.

Lambert turned and shuffled out back into the light and handed the pendant to Theodore, who gazed at it in wonder. 'You didn't disturb them, did you?' he asked.

'No – I left them exactly as I found them,' Lambert lied.

19

The Night Hunt

~ and haunting howls ~

Christian Hayter looked out from one of the train's small darkened windows at the golden sunset and landscape outside. 'It's not right,' he muttered to himself.

'What's not right?' Bishop replied, thinking it was directed at him.

'Not being in charge.' Hayter glared out of the window.

'In charge of what?' Bishop asked and stood a little closer.

'I was once in charge of a busy trade in exotic Raptor of Paradise feathers, the governor of a small group of islands in Indonesia. Had my own tyrant and rode it around like a king. Then *they* arrived. Out of the blue, starting to ask questions about a little incident a long time ago, and it all fell apart.' Hater scowled at his reflection.

'I thought you said this was a promotion, and that that hot, sticky island was getting too small for you?' Bishop said, puzzled.

Hayter turned and cut him a sharp look that should

have instantly changed the tone of conversation, but Bishop pushed on. 'The Doctor told me the Viscount's wife has lost interest in feathers; they're no longer in fashion. It's all about beauty products now – creams and lotions to make you look younger.'

'So I'm told, Bishop,' Hayter replied.

'Boss – hope you don't mind me asking,' said Bishop, 'but what does the Doctor do all day in that laboratory? You know, the carriage we're not allowed to go in?'

'Your guess is as good as mine,' Hayter said curtly.

'Ash and I were wondering,' Bishop continued, 'what's with the tyrants the Doctor secretly keeps away from here? I'm not too happy about helping him with his night feeds. He gives me the creeps, and those tyrants are unstable. I don't want to end up like those last two assistants of his . . .'

Hayter stepped back from the window. 'I'd try not to ask too many questions, Bishop, and do as you're told.' But Hayter could see that the questions would not stop. 'Look, if you must know, the Viscount has some sort of big plan for the Doctor's pet tyrants, and for the glands we've been cutting out from all the saurs we've killed for the past year. Now he needs us here to personally oversee his secret operations in America and work alongside him.'

The train jolted and started to move off slowly.

'If we just follow orders and keep out of trouble – and stay alive, we'll soon find out what this is all about,' Hayter added.

'I think I preferred our old life back on Aru,' Bishop lamented, 'with you giving the orders, not taking them, boss.'

Hayter raised his eyebrows. 'I know what you mean, Bishop. Now look at me: I'm on the night shift babysitting a demented doctor.'

'Demented . . . I shall take that as a compliment.'

Hayter and Bishop turned round quickly to face the Doctor, who stood at the end of the carriage dressed in a black suit and white apron that was splattered with blood. His black hair was slicked back and he wore darkened round glasses.

'Thank you, Mr Hayter, for joining me on a night hunt,' he said in measured tones, with the trace of an accent. 'I hope it is not an inconvenience.'

'No, no, it's not,' Hayter replied quickly.

'Excellent,' the Doctor said. 'The Viscount has told me you're good with saurs.'

Hayter nodded, flattered.

'Good, then we shall be on our way. My tyrants will be hungry, and we have work to do. Please, would you lower the window shutters, as we must travel in darkness. No one must see us – or where I keep them.'

'I had wondered where they were hiding,' Hayter said.

'I can't keep them cooped up on a train all day, not after the last incident. We will pick some up and have a little fun with them.' The Doctor let out a chilling laugh

and smiled. 'Now, if you don't mind, I have work to do.'

The Doctor clicked his heels and went back from where he came. The train shunted forward and slowly moved off into the darkness.

* * *

Unlike well-used old trains, the Viscount's well-oiled train uttered no squeaks and squeals as it gently slowed down with its brakes – but when it pulled to a stop it lurched with a jolt, knocking Hayter slightly off balance.

Everyone disembarked and made their way to the back of the train in the darkness to where the new livestock carriages had been coupled. The long side door slid silently open to reveal the Doctor smiling in the moonlight. He now wore a long black riding coat with black gloves. He was still wearing his darkened round glasses, even though it was completely dark outside.

'Gentlemen, let's do a spot of hunting,' he declared. 'But first, Mr Ash and Mr Bishop, would you please help with the ramp?'

Hayter moved aside as the boarding ramp was lowered. He walked up to where the Doctor stood.

'There are saddled allosaurs in this carriage ready for you to follow my tyrants, who are in the next carriage,' the Doctor told him. 'I will be close behind in the truck with the others. Be warned: they are quite excited, so hang well back while they hunt, or it will be you they turn on. Once they have made their kill, you'll step in before they make too much mess, and extract the glands. We don't want them eating what we've come here for, do we?' The Doctor laughed to himself.

Hayter smiled a little uncomfortably. 'So you want me to jump in front of some frenzied feasting tyrants that you have trained to be vicious killers and make them stop eating? I'm good with saurs, but not that good. You're not seriously asking me to do that? It's suicide.'

'Trust me, Mr Hayter,' the Doctor replied brusquely. 'I've been working out here with my tyrants for close to six months now. We've been doing this almost every night. I have ways to make my tyrants do as I please. Admittedly the last people helping got a little too close . . . but I'm told you're a professional. You just need to roll up your sleeves and follow my orders, exactly to the letter, and without question.'

Hayter bit his lip and silently mounted his allosaur while reluctantly awaiting his next order. The Doctor didn't fuss about, and soon the next carriage door swooshed open and out bound four large tyrants, which shook their ragged feathers, stretched out their legs, and circled round.

'Aren't they magnificent?' the Doctor called to Hayter.

'I can't even make out what type they are,' Hayter said.

'Those two golden ones are Lythronax – similar to the Ronax you acquired in Africa, but they live in the mountains – and the shaggy ones are just plain Brown Tyrants. They still have some of last year's coat and it's coming off in clumps. They were all reared together,' the Doctor went on. 'The Lythronax are more dominant than the Brown Tyrants, who would normally hunt alone, but being reared together they all work as a pack.'

'Impressive,' Hayter said. 'These all of them?'

'No,' the Doctor replied. 'I have three other packs in training.'

Hayter gulped. 'How long have you been doing this?'

'All my life. My father kept carnotors in the Black Forest,' he said. 'I inherited his skills, and together we trained them to fight in the war.'

Hayter looked at the Doctor with a raised level of respect. 'Berserka saurs?' he yelped. 'You trained the feared berserkas?'

The Doctor nodded. 'You can ask questions later, Mr Hayter,' he said. 'It looks like the tyrants have a scent, so we'd better follow.' He quickly led his allosaur down the ramp and into the darkness.

'You okay, boss?' Bishop asked, waiting behind with Ash.

'I was right,' Hayter said. 'He's a demented doctor all right. We'd better catch up, lads – stay close and do as he says; we'll learn a lot from this man.'

And with that the three of them sped off into the night.

✦ ✦ ✦

Unlike the Ronax in Africa, which yelped like dogs, the Lythronax let out long and haunting howls like wolves. The Brown Tyrants panted a lot of the time, and when called they replied with a low howl-like imitation. The Doctor said that it was merely simulating the more dominant Lythronax, and that they would normally only make noises when calling for a mate in the desolate expanse of the land and the mountain ranges that divided the states of California and Nevada. Of course, Hayter knew that most tyrants around the world now lived in reserves or in captivity, like all predators larger than humans. So following the pack at night was a very special task, and wasn't too hard to do if you listened out for the strange mix of eerie howls.

It wasn't long before the beasts had circled and set upon a group of unsuspecting tritops that didn't stand a chance against the might and ferocity of the coordinated attack. By the time the humans got close, the larger Lythronax was taking down a second, older tritops, while the other three tucked in to their dinner. The sound of chomping and crunching was intense.

'Gentlemen,' the Doctor announced, 'you all did exceptionally well collecting samples for me in Kenya, so collect the tritops' glands in the same way.'

Ash put up his hand like a schoolboy in class. 'Excuse me, sir,' he said cautiously. 'When we shot the Krugers in Kenya, they were not being eaten by tyrants at the time.'

Hayter and Bishop both looked intently at the Doctor, who dismounted in one quick move and retrieved a torch from his pocket while striding towards the tyrants.

One of them let out a high-pitched bark that drew the attention of the others, as they all lifted their glistening, bloodied heads into the moonlight and stared directly at the man.

Hayter gently pulled the reins on his allosaur and readied himself for a quick turn in case this went horribly wrong.

The Doctor swiftly lifted his dark glasses and shone the torch straight into his left eye. It somehow reflected back out into the night with sparkles of fine reds, blues and purples. The tyrants all suddenly stood upright and alert, quivering. Hayter, Ash and Bishop stared on, half mesmerised and half in disbelief.

The Doctor stepped boldly forward a few paces, and the reaction from the tyrants was instant as they recoiled, tripping backwards to get away. A few more paces and the Doctor was at the first slain tritops.

'I suggest, Mr Hayter,' he commanded, 'you pull up those sleeves of yours and retrieve those glands – we don't want you getting blood on your shirt, do we?'

20

The Stricken Zino

~ and Matti the bear ~

Carter crept up the pathway in the dark. The moon had sunk below the horizon but millions of stars were enough to light the way. The cry was faint, but he was sure it was coming from up ahead where the rock face became ragged again. He turned a corner and saw another mine entrance, this time with broken boards – and it was open. He crept up and in. There was a strange welcoming red light coming from deeper within the mine, and silhouetted in front of it was a large slumped creature. It moved slightly towards Carter, slowly raised a forelimb, and cried out in pain. It was a feathered saur of huge proportions, with a long thin neck and small beaked head. At the end of its forelimbs were the longest claws Carter had ever seen, each as long as its legs. Thankfully it wasn't waving them about defensively, but reclined in an uncomfortable position. As Carter edged closer, he felt his feet become wet and with the next step, he suddenly slipped into a deep pool of cold water. He bobbed up, coughing and spluttering, and grappled to get back to the edge. Disorientated from the darkness, he desperately felt his way out of the cold water and flopped into the warm comfort of the strange creature's deep plumage. Carter's heart was racing from the shock of going under, but now he was wrapped up next to this strange saur in the darkness, and could feel its heart beating. He was safe for now. They remained that way until Carter dropped off to sleep.

◆ ◆ ◆

'Uncle Cash!' Carter called, returning to the campsite at first light. 'Come quickly! There's an injured saur who needs our help!' He shook his uncle awake.

'She's been bitten,' Carter told him. 'She's been calling for her mate but he's not returned. Something terrible has happened and she needs protection – and a nest.'

Cash looked at his nephew in alarm. 'You're covered in blood!' he exclaimed.

Carter looked down at his hands, which were red with the saur's blood, and small downy white feathers were stuck to the sticky substance. Beyond that, his wet body was a more orange-red, just like the mountainous hills around them. 'I fell in some water,' he explained. 'The mine is filled with water, so the saur couldn't hide any deeper.'

'Red water!' Cash exclaimed, then looked puzzled. 'Why a nest?'

Carter rubbed his tummy. 'All females need a nest for eggs.'

'How long do we have?' said Wolf, who was standing there in the dim light.

Carter shrugged. 'I only know about Shadow Raptor nests. Never seen this saur before. She's a lot bigger. Sometimes, if a raptor nest is disturbed, the female can hold on to eggs inside her until there's a safer time to lay, but not long. Eggs must come out.'

Carter showed them where she was hiding in the old mine. As soon as Cash caught a glimpse in the lantern light, he gasped. Before him was a saur so elusive he'd imagined them extinct.

'We could try to make it back to the Washoe reservation,' suggested Wolf.

'No. Best we get back to my ranch,' Cash said. 'Finding out what's making the water run red will have to wait. This is a Great Zino – perhaps the last of its kind – so she must be kept alive at all costs, and her eggs protected. Whatever attacked her is still out there.'

'She can hardly walk,' said Carter.

Cash thought for a moment. 'The old mining cart, back at the mine entrance where we met you, Wolf. We could get her onto that.'

'My horse is fastest; I'll be back soon with it,' Wolf said, and darted off back down the pathway.

Cash looked at Carter. 'She could fit on the cart, but

how do we get her onto it?'

'Communication, remember?' Carter replied.

✦ ✦ ✦

Cash watched as his nephew stood calmly in front of the Great Zino until she settled enough to focus on him. There appeared to be not a lot of movement of any kind, except that Carter seemed to be breathing not just deeply, but obviously. He was over-inflating his chest, almost exaggerating its expansion, so that the rhythm of his breathing could be seen, heard and even felt. Cash closed his eyes and held his hands over his ears, and for a short while focused his senses. He could somehow feel Carter's breathing, and his calm presence. He released his ears and opened his eyes so that all his senses came alive, and realised that he was breathing in perfect sync with Carter, and so was the zino. Whatever Carter was doing, it was affecting everything around him. The boy was right – there were other ways to communicate, beyond sight and sound.

The Great Zino raised herself, lifting her cramped forelimbs wide and revealing the true scale of her huge feathered mass and the extraordinary length of her enormous claws. Carter was very close by and easily within striking distance, but didn't flinch. Instead he reached out and inquisitively ran his right hand along the three slightly curved claws. In any other situation, Cash would have jumped in and dragged the boy away,

but instead he watched and marvelled at the creature with respect.

The zino opened up her beak and made a little gargling noise that Carter mimicked back perfectly.

Cash stepped backwards out of the mine, as together in perfect synchrony the saur and boy moved into the daylight.

Wolf had returned with the cart as promised, and turned to Cash. 'It's not perfect but will do. Help me secure her.'

Carter gently helped the zino take painful steps forward on her bleeding leg. But when the zino saw Buster and Looper she froze, which Carter was quick to notice. He gave both the carnivores a glance that made them turn and ignore what was going on. The zino was still cautious, and hesitated just beyond the mine entrance, so Carter barked at the other two saurs. This made them gently trot away a good few paces, and calmly sit down, facing away. Cash looked towards Wolf, who raised another eyebrow with appreciation. It was clear that Carter could will the saurs to do as he wished. It was simply achieved without effort or fuss, and the saurs all obeyed. The command Carter sent out demanded the allo and tyrant to become passive and docile, and the zino to be brave and overcome her fear and pain. All three were at ease, and Carter slowly helped the zino over to the cart.

Wolf and Cash braced the front as the stricken zino slumped onto it with a thud. Carter then helped lift her short but densely feathered tail, taking his time to fold and make good her stray feathers. This, after all, is what any self-respecting feathered creature would do, and he knew this first-hand.

Wolf had gathered up all their blankets and tucked them around the stricken saur, who was now at ease around the humans. The sun was now fully risen and the morning was well underway. Wolf walked alongside his horse, making sure the cart was secure and being dragged behind, as they moved off.

They hadn't gone far when an enormous bear lunged out from the treeline and bound over towards them on all fours, then reared up, standing tall on its hind legs and letting out a defiant roar. The startled horse and saurs all froze.

'Down!' Wolf cried out to it. 'I'm busy, can't you see?' He stepped from the cart and moved towards the bear. 'These are friends of mine.'

Cash and Carter looked on with open mouths. The bear stood over ten feet tall and continued to roar, but Wolf just walked up to it boldly and rubbed its belly. He shrugged and turned to Cash and Carter, saying, 'Sorry – the bear does not mean to frighten you again.'

'I thought you couldn't speak bear?' Carter asked.

'I can't, and he can't speak Washoe either,' Wolf

explained. 'That's why he gets confused. This is Matti the bear; he has been with me since he was a cub.'

'He's your pet?' asked Cash, astonished.

Wolf gave Cash a stare and said, 'I'm glad he cannot understand English as he would not like you saying that.'

'Is this the same bear that attacked us yesterday?' asked Carter.

Wolf looked about apologetically and patted Matti on the back with enough force to make him come down from his high pose and back onto all fours with a mighty thud.

'I'm sorry we scared you,' he said.

21

The Sting

~ a perfectly brilliant idea ~

From the docks Bea could see an impressive structure taking shape over the San Francisco Bay – the new Golden Gate Bridge. Alcatraz Island, and the prison on it, was hazy on the horizon. San Francisco had lived up to Bea's expectations and was very different from the other cities she had visited. The city's hills had caught her attention first: the very steep inclines and descents, with houses painted in different colours built in steps that ran alongside the steep sidewalks. Then there were the cable cars, beautifully decorated, providing access to everywhere in the city, although Bea and her cousins hadn't been able to persuade Anya to let them go on one, as she preferred to travel in her chauffeur-driven car.

Bea was happy to do her part to put an end to the raptor black market, even if it meant pretending to be Anya's spoilt daughter. She had witnessed the start of this trade back in Aru, and had even freed a cargo of raptors that were destined for cities like this with the help of her brother.

'Ah! How could I possibly miss you!' said a horrid stocky little man who was wearing an ill-fitting suit. Bea looked him up and down with disdain. If Christian Hayter had an American brother, this would be him. Loathsome.

'You're on time,' said Anya crisply. 'Where are the saurs? I can't stand this place, so let's be quick.'

'I have one over here,' the man grunted, and pointed to an empty sack draped over a small cage. Before he could fully reveal it, Anya blew her top.

'Was I not clear enough on the telephone earlier?' She spat the words out venomously and pointed to the cage. 'Whatever that is, take it away, and don't waste our time.' Anya scooped up Bea's arm, turned round and forcibly headed back to the car.

The man was caught off guard. 'Hang on, wait – I can show you more,' he called out after them.

Bea tugged her arm free from Anya and stomped back to the man.

'Mama promised me I could choose one. I want to see them all.' She stamped her foot, crossed her arms, and stared at the man. Bea was roused by Anya's confidence and drew upon recollections of her younger self who had been, as she now realised, very spoilt by her grandmother.

Anya strode back up the dock, still attracting the eyes of all the workers who milled about.

'This is my daughter, and if you think I'm tough, wait until you deal with her,' she spat. 'Now listen: she wants to

see all of them and choose one – perhaps a few – whatever she wants.' She slowly leant in close to the man and poked him in the chest. 'And don't try any more tricks or funny business,' she cautioned.

'Sorry – I have to be careful,' whispered the man, 'selling exotic saurs. We don't want to attract the wrong sort of people, such as the police.'

'Oh – don't worry about the police,' Anya replied breezily, 'my husband has them in his back pocket.' She waved off his comments. 'Between you and me, we're above the law – so can we get on? My patience is thin, and, I fear, so is my daughter's.'

The man quickly walked a short distance up a jetty to a large listing cargo boat that looked like its days afloat were numbered. He gestured for them to follow up the gangplank and come inside. They were greeted by a Chinese man who was shocked to see such glamour on his deck.

'There are literally a million places I would rather be than here,' Anya said loudly. 'Please show my daughter all of your saurs – every last one of them. NOW.'

The man waved some people over and said something, before directing them to another part of the boat that housed a multitude of cages. A putrid smell of fur and feathers hung in the foetid air.

Bea walked into the middle of the cabin and saw all manner of creatures, all in a distressed state. The good, wholesome Bea silently fumed with rage. 'I WANT A SHADOW RAPTOR!' she yelled, and stamped her foot for good measure.

The men looked at each other, bemused by this young girl's rudeness as Anya rushed to speak with the Chinese man, who ran over and bowed.

'Apologies, we have no Shadow Raptors,' he said. 'All Raptor of Paradise trade has stopped; we can't get any more. This is the very last cargo of exotic saurs. The supply ran dry about a year ago. Since then we have not been able to get any. Please, this is all we have.' He bowed again and stepped back to give her space.

Bea looked at the man . . . looked at Anya . . . looked at all the people who were all involved in this black market trade who had gathered to see this spoiled brat choose a saur for a pet. She then turned to see all the cages filled with sorry-looking half-dead creatures, and announced, 'I want them ALL.'

The man's eyes lit up. 'Of course,' he said, nodding.

Bea then pulled out a shiny whistle that a nice policeman had given her earlier, put it to her lips, and blew as hard as she could.

Almost immediately a cavalcade of uniformed officers burst into the cabin, and true to his word, Monty was there, dressed as a policeman alongside them.

'They let me borrow the uniform,' he whispered to Bea conspiratorially. 'Okay, I pretended I was researching a new role. Gimme a break.' He winked, and Bea smiled.

'I'm glad you're not dressed as Tarzan,' she confided. Beside her sat the cage still with the sack on top. She lifted it and found another beautiful Raptor of Paradise inside it – thin, shaking and in a sorry state indeed.

Anya, still in character, rushed over. 'Now that you have one, can we please go shopping?' she pleaded. 'This dress is simply ruined.' She started to guide Bea outside.

Monty stopped her. 'Anya, you were great. All that demanding, and stuff about having the police in your pocket – great improvisation, totally amazing. Had everyone believing you were the real deal. Horrid, stuck up, rich . . . You know what I mean.' He gave her a wink.

'What can I say, I was born for this role,' Anya said curtly, and stormed off outside.

'Wow,' Monty remarked. 'Her and Lambert . . . that I got to see.'

May and Violet had been hiding nervously along with Micki, and rushed over as soon as it was safe.

As Micki snapped away, she said, 'I can't wait to show my editors – what a great exposé this will make!'

'A real-life sting on a ruthless gang of black market saur traders with a Hollywood star,' quipped Violet.

Her sister sighed. 'It's simply the best trip ever.'

Micki's flashbulb blew and there, in the next day's morning paper, delivered to the Grand Hotel, was the image of Anya and Bea standing next to Monty on the

dockside, holding a Raptor of Paradise. Above the image read the headline 'Saving the Saurs: Monty Lomax, Hero of Undercover Raid'.

During checkout, the concierge recognised Anya and asked for an autograph. This thrilled her to bits, and for a brief moment she smiled. The chief of police was waiting on the steps of the hotel to thank them personally.

'So you're the kid who knows Monty,' he enthused to Bea. 'He's a great guy. Finally we've been able to throw the whole gang in jail – all thanks to you girls.' He mimed locking a door and throwing a key away over his shoulder. 'We heard the whole conversation and are confident we've closed their black market trade once and for all in this great city. We have all the saurs on a truck, plus the one that Hector had in his store.'

Bea and the twins all smiled warmly.

Bea spoke up first. 'What will happen to them now?' she asked.

'I'm afraid they'll have to be put down, young lady,' the chief of police said regretfully. 'Obviously we can't sell them, and they are in pretty bad shape. It's the best thing for them at the end of the day.'

'But we saved them!' Bea said hotly. 'Surely that wasn't in vain!'

'I'm sorry,' the chief of police replied, 'but –'

Bea cut him off before he could utter another word. 'We'll take them!' she cried. 'We have a ranch where they can be looked after, and experts who know just how to do it!'

'Yes, yes, yes!' the twins joined in. 'Oh, DO let us – please?'

'Well, I can't just turn them over without adult consent, now, ladies,' the chief of police demurred.

Anya finally found her moment to win Bea over for good. 'I think it's a perfectly brilliant idea,' she said brightly. 'You have my full permission. I'll arrange for them to be transported immediately.'

The three girls all looked at each other, stunned.

22

Sidney and Bunty

~ a stowaway boy ~

Theodore shuddered as it grew darker and colder in the ravine. 'I suggest we camp here tonight,' he said.

Lambert looked about. 'Here? In this graveyard?'

'It's late and well sheltered, so why not?' Theodore buttoned up his jacket. 'I'll lead the allosaurs down the easy way. I believe a branch off the old tree is somewhere amongst that pile of bones.' He pointed. 'Can you gather some wood so I can start us a fire and cook us up a tin or two of SPAW?'

Lambert looked horrified. 'Seriously,' he blurted. 'SPAW? Have you nothing better?'

Theodore grabbed the end of the rope that he'd tossed down and started to make his way back up. 'You said that you were the outdoors type,' he called over his shoulder. 'I'm not asking you to sing round the campfire – just get warm and eat.'

'I've camped out in worse places, but with better food,' Lambert replied. 'I know what goes into SPAW, you know – I own the Sauria Canning Company.'

Theodore was unmoved. 'You can gnaw on one of these old bones with the allosaurs if you prefer. Now it's getting dark, so let's get a move on.'

+ + +

Theodore was true to his word, and in no time he came back and let the allosaurs sniff around while he got a fire going. Lambert was proud of the pile of very dry wood that had taken some effort to excavate. The whole process had been overshadowed with the knowledge that he was very much alone, and that if Theodore had an accident or rode away on purpose, Lambert might spend the rest of his short life here, becoming the third human skeleton to join the thousands of other saurs in this grim graveyard.

They both silently got on with the job at hand and it was not until the boiled tin of mixed saurmeat was opened that Theodore said anything. 'I always found SPAW to be quite salty, but it was the only thing available during the war and quite a luxury. Most of the time provisions were so low that the army resorted to eating dried SPAX – you know, the dried allo food that comes in barrels.'

'The Sauria Canning Company also makes SPAX,' Lambert said. 'It's made from all the SPAW leftovers not fit for humans. We used to dump it all, but I noticed that the wild saurs came at night to feed on it. Not wanting to waste a fortune, I got a very clever food chemist to develop it into a healthy dried animal feed. He worked out that

even the bone could be baked and crumbled into SPAX.' Lambert looked quite pleased with himself.

Theodore found a bit of gristle between his teeth and felt a little squirmy.

'He revolutionised my company,' Lambert went on, 'and discovered many more uses for every part of a saur, including its offal and glands, which are all now highly profitable. The man is a genius.'

'Surely feeding saurs with the leftovers of other saurs is wrong?' Theodore questioned, but realised he had not entirely got his point across.

'Not *that* wrong, my friend,' Lambert replied. 'Allosaurs and other carnivores eat other saurs. They eat everything. The meat, guts and bone. It's not that different opening a tin and feeding it the same stuff with a bit of salt thrown in as a preservative.'

'But SPAX is also used as a feed for herbivores – and that's wrong,' Theodore pointed out. 'I was raised in a saurmonger's. I ate the leftovers, but inedible rotten meat was always tossed away, we'd never have fed it to the saurs.'

Lambert maintained his position. 'SPAX is full of nutrients and rich in minerals. Okay, perhaps it needs to be rebranded, as sales are not what they used to be.'

Theodore pondered the second tin of SPAW that had been bathed in a pan of hot water, and closely read the label.

Lambert saw his dilemma. 'Go on, open it,' he said. 'I

was being a snob – there's nothing wrong with SPAW or any of my products.'

'Yes,' Theodore said warily, 'but what type of saur goes into "mixed saurmeat", and why isn't it listed on the label?'

'Good question. It depends on where it's canned, you see. Before refrigeration we had to slaughter, butcher, cook and can the meat all in the same day. Most of the canning factories around the world have a variety of different saurs in the slaughterhouse so the contents are always mixed. For example, in Mexico we have a lot of rubeos – the stytops with the long nose horn and brow horns – and the smaller apatos with the long neck spines. So it's all mixed up. In Africa we have a lot of Red Stytops – not that tasty, so we mix kylos with it. The trick is to add salt, lots of salt – and eventually it all tastes the same no matter where it's canned or what saurs it's made from.'

Theodore lifted the tin out of the water with a gloved hand. 'So do you know what this can has in it?'

Lambert smiled and nodded. 'It has a red label; that's produced locally, so it's definitely prime tritops, probably from a rancher Cash knows.'

Theodore raised his eyebrows. 'Well, I would definitely open it if the little key to wind it open was still attached!'

Lambert laughed and shrugged his shoulders. 'And I would join you – tritops are very tasty.'

Theodore whipped out his knife and jabbed it into the side of the tin, letting out a whistle of hot steam, and started to work his way round the edge.

'You know, getting a tin with a missing key happens quite a lot. I should write to the owner one day and complain!'

Lambert, however, missed the joke. Instead his face froze. 'Your knife – what's that set in the end?'

Theodore looked down and realised the one secret he had been keeping from Lambert was sparkling in the dim flickering light like a cluster of fireflies. 'You know what it is, Lambert,' he said reluctantly. 'A keystone.'

'You had a keystone all this time?' Lambert said in disbelief, as Theodore carried on opening the tin. 'Then why did you need the remaining twin's keystone? It should be mine – I'm the one who retrieved it,' he reasoned.

Theodore silently pulled off the top of the tin, and with the knife lopped half of the SPAW onto Lambert's tin plate and handed it to him before replying.

'For a long time I believed that Franklin should never have taken one of the twin's keystones,' Theodore said, blowing on the meat to cool it. 'It was the start of Frank's long obsession with the Saurmen and what led to his and Grace's deaths. Then I read some of his older journals in an attempt to find out where he went missing. I learnt that having been given a keystone meant you were able to find other people with keystones, and find the hidden temples. So it was actually all my fault, and I started to blame myself for leading him here in the first place.' He took a tentative bite of SPAW from his knife before continuing.

'Now I've realised that I was supposed to lead Franklin here, and he was supposed to take the twin's keystone. You've read his last journal, so you know that his very last entry stated that he wanted to give his keystone to his new son, Carter.'

Lambert spoke up. 'Yes, he told me that.'

'You see it was Carter's destiny to wear it,' Theodore explained, 'but this sadly never happened. His rightful keystone is still with Franklin and Grace, wherever their remains are scattered in Aru. *This* keystone –' Theodore held it up in the flickering firelight so it could dazzle – 'is the other half of the stone Franklin wore. It's not the next-best thing; it's the same thing. The twins are joined together; they are two halves of the same thing – and so are their keystones. Castor and Pollux, he called them, after the two brightest stars in the sky that night, in the constellation of Gemini – the twins.'

Theodore could see that Lambert finally understood the huge importance of the dazzling object.

'This is Carter's keystone,' Theodore said firmly.

Lambert silently nodded and swallowed the salty saurmeat. 'So who gave you *your* keystone?' he asked.

'Now that's another story for another day.'

Theodore wiped the jellied meat residue off the knife's blade and carefully placed it back into its sheath.

'You can't silence my curiosity that easily,' Lambert protested. 'You have a keystone and forgot to mention it?'

'Well, Saurmen don't brag about their keystones,' Theodore said. 'Like you said, it's a well-kept secret.' Theodore could not help but feel immensely proud to finally say the words and mean it.

'So it was your stone that found this temple tree and the twins,' Lambert asserted.

'Must have been – if Frank's research is to be believed, that is,' Theodore replied.

'Tell me, how was the keystone passed to you – and more to the point by whom?' Lambert was not going to let the details slip away, so Theodore took a hot mouthful and pondered his reply.

'I was a boy, not much older than Carter,' he said slowly. 'Some kids were robbing a man close to the saurmonger's my father owned in the East End of London. I stopped them – don't know why, I just did – though not on my own – Champion, the phalox that practically brought me up, did all the work. The kids ran off after a good head-butting. I helped the man up, and there it was, hanging round his neck. It was the most beautiful thing I had ever seen.'

Lambert jumped in. 'And he just gave it to you?'

'No – I made sure he was okay, and walked with him for a while to check that the gang of thugs and pickpockets weren't following. But a year later I was at the docks, waiting for a cargo of saurmeat. You are aware of the black market saurmeat trade, I presume?' he said sarcastically, shooting Lambert a quick look.

Lambert nodded. 'There's probably a boy like you at every dock around the world. The black market happens everywhere.'

'Well, I saw the gentleman again,' Theodore said. 'He was overseeing some cargo being loaded onto the same ship, the *Enterprise*. He was with a kindly-looking woman and a young girl, and with them was a magnificent megalosaur. I was spellbound. They eventually boarded the ship, but I stayed in the shadows. I watched my contact sell his black market meat and leave. By then, it was the middle of the night, and as the deckhands started to load the cargo and the megalosaur onto the ship, I joined in. I grabbed one of the crates, stepped off the dock, and walked on board. I didn't return to England until I came back to serve in the war.'

Lambert was rapt. 'So you left England to follow the man with the keystone – where to?'

'I stowed away. I never even said goodbye to my father and brothers. It wasn't an especially warm household to grow up in. I guess I had an adventurous streak and saw my opportunity. Ten days later we were in New York.'

'Remarkable,' Lambert uttered. 'So when did this gentleman give you the keystone?'

'I lasted the whole journey on scraps the megalosaur left me. I basically slept in the hold with it,' Theodore said,

shaking his head at the memory. 'On the last morning, when we docked, customs agents found me. I had no papers, nothing. Then there he was, the gentleman and his lovely wife, paying a large amount of money to have them find some paperwork for me. One minute I was destined for the return trip home and a beating from my father; the next I'm in America starting a new life in the new world.'

'Why did he pay off the officials?' Lambert asked.

'Apparently he knew all along I was there – he overfed the megalosaur with prime cooked meat from the kitchens, knowing I was eating it as well. Puts SPAX to shame, I must say.'

'And did he know who you were?' Lambert asked.

'Yes, he knew exactly who I was. I'd saved him a year earlier, and he saved me in return. He said it was destiny that our paths had crossed. We were meant to meet each other and he was meant to pass something on to me – the sparkling stone he wore round his neck.'

'So this gentleman willingly gave his keystone to a stowaway boy.' Lambert sucked air between his teeth. 'Did he know how precious it was?'

'He never told me much about it other than I had to respect it and the saurs I met on my path in life. He also said that one day it would call to me, and I would then know what the stone was for. I was just mesmerised by how beautiful it was, and how this one strange object had somehow already changed my life in ways I could have never guessed. A few years later, I set it into this knife, and it has never left my side.'

'Amazing,' Lambert murmured. 'And whatever happened to the man?'

Theodore breathed in deeply, before he said sadly, 'Sidney was everything to me, and so was his wife, Bunty.'

The Viscount sat back so that the firelight left his face and it sank into the darkness. 'Barbara and Sidney Brownlee,' he muttered, then leant back into the light from the fire. 'Dear Bunty, dear, dear, Bunty – it's so sad. I knew her so briefly, just like Franklin and Grace. Now I understand why you were so close to her, Theodore. Tell me, who else have you told this story to?'

'No one – not even Franklin knew.' Theodore looked to the ground.

'Good,' declared Lambert. 'I mean, who but me would understand?'

23

Doctor Klaus Achtecka

~ the how and the why ~

By dawn, Hayter, Ash and Bishop had harvested eleven prime tritop glands from twelve kills. One tyrant had torn a calf's head clean off in a rage and had made a mess of the neck so it was left as a half-eaten

lump. The confusing mix of teeth and claw marks from two different tyrants would make it hard to work out what exactly had killed them, and the knife marks used by the humans were impossible to notice amongst the mess. The swiftness of the tyrant's surprise night attacks meant the tritops had no time to resist or run, so they died where they rested for the night. The men brushed away the tyrant and human footprints then dragged branches behind the allosaurs to further cover their tracks. As each hunt had taken place miles apart, anyone would have thought that these were all individual but strangely identical incidents.

The men all resisted the temptation to ask the Doctor how he managed to control the tyrants to such effect, and what it was he kept hidden behind his darkened glasses. The Doctor was always direct and polite in administering his orders and each hunt was run with military precision. Hayter observed the Doctor intently and saw that he had an air of confidence and authority that pretty much willed the saurs and humans to do as he wanted. Whatever the Doctor was doing to his berserka saurs was somehow rubbing off on them all. There were no verbal or physical commands; all the Doctor did was shine the light into his eye. It clearly provided another inaudible command telling the tyrants exactly what to do after he'd commanded their attention.

◆ ◆ ◆

Dawn's rays were streaking across the sky as the train trundled back to the deserted siding from which they had set off at dusk. Towelling his arms after washing off the blood, Hayter ambled into the next carriage to have a moment alone with the man for whom he had a new-found respect.

'Thank you Doctor,' Hayter said, 'that was what I've been missing for a long time.'

'What have you been missing, Mr Hayter?' the Doctor asked.

'You know, a proper bit of dirty work – hunting, being around well-trained tyrants.'

'Thank you, Mr Hayter,' the Doctor replied. 'I know a compliment from you is a rare thing. I also know you probably have questions you want to ask.'

'Yes, I do,' Hayter admitted, sensing his opportunity. 'I was hoping you could help me. You see, I had a tyrant once – a Black Dwarf from Flores. I thought I had it under control; even had a saddle made for it and rode it around. Sadly it was taken from me.'

'I think I had the pleasure of seeing this tyrant the other day at the county fair,' announced the Doctor. 'I was surprised by one all the way over here in America. So I had to take a good look at it, with my eye.' He tapped the blackened lens of his glasses. 'Turns out our employer was there to see my powers up close.' The Doctor grinned to himself. 'The Viscount told me it was once yours, and that you had managed to train it to be ridden. That's a very difficult thing to achieve. I'm impressed.'

'Thank you,' Hayter replied, still furious about the idea that his tyrant had managed to end up here, of all places.

'Not even I have ridden a tyrant, Mr Hayter. They're too unpredictable and uncomfortable. Are they not too wide on the hips?'

'I used this.' Hayter pulled out his bullhook and ran his finger along the sinister metal curved hook at the top of a black and silver inlaid shaft. 'I keep the head well polished,' he explained. 'It's good at catching the tyrant's attention and reminding it of the pain it inflicts. Tyrants are sensitive here –' Hayter rubbed the base of his neck –

'and a little tap or two keeps it aware that I'm in charge when mounted on its back.'

The Doctor exhaled. 'Interesting . . . very interesting. As I understand it, your tyrant was taken by a boy – but there was a girl riding it at the fair.'

'That would be his stuck-up sister,' Hayter spat, feeling a rage burn inside him. 'The boy was found living feral with Shadow Raptors. He managed to turn my tyrant on me. And now he rides it bareback – as if it's easy to do. No training, no bother – can do it just like that.' Hayter clicked his fingers.

The Doctor turned in contemplation to Hayter and ran his hand over his slicked-back hair. 'Tell me, Mr Hayter, does he have one of these?' And with that he lifted his darkened glasses to reveal that his left eye was made from an odd black stone in which minute flecks of dazzling bright colour danced.

Hayter's eyes widened. It looked so haunting; he was nervous about staring at it, but felt compelled to at the same time. 'No,' he said. 'What exactly is that?'

The Doctor replaced his glasses before explaining.

'I lost an eye as a child,' he said brusquely. 'It was an accident. A carnotor's horn poked it out.'

Hayter winced at the thought.

'My father had this strange stone,' the Doctor continued. 'I understand it's some sort of opal. He smoothed it down into a sphere just the right size to use as a replacement eye.'

Hayter peered more closely. 'What, you can see with it?'

The Doctor laughed out loud. 'That would be nice, but no. It was just to fill the socket with something that the other boys would not tease me for. It did the trick – even spooked them. No one messed with the boy from the Black Forest with the evil eye, that was for certain.'

Hayter nodded. 'But I don't understand – how does your stone eye work?'

'I don't fully understand *how*, Mr Hayter, and I am not too bothered in the *why* either. What I do know is that the stone somehow works on saurs, and I can project with my mind what it is I want them to do.'

'So you've been able to do this since you were a child, like the raptor boy?' Hayter asked, still struggling with the how and the why.

'No,' the Doctor replied. 'I have had to work at this.' He drummed his fingers on the carriage's table. 'After a few years I started noticing saurs feared me when I stared at them. I slowly took advantage of this, and then discovered I could really hurt them, inside their minds, just by thinking it. Where I lived, the forests were full of carnotors. I would go out to practise my skills on them all the time. I literally blew their minds.' The Doctor demonstrated with his fingers, mimicking an explosion near his temples. 'This gave me plenty of saurs to cut open and experiment on, and I ended up being one of the top organic chemists in the world.'

'So you're a scientist or vet type of doctor then?' asked Hayter.

The Doctor smiled coldly. 'I like to take saurs apart, not put them back together.'

'Ash and Bishop reckon that it was your berserka saurs that everyone feared in the war,' Hayter prodded.

'My reputation travels well. The truth is my legion of berserkas killed more German soldiers than English ones, as they would savage anything in their path. The propaganda told a different story. Some top people in the army discovered my skills, and advanced my experimentation to a whole new level. After the war I had to lay low, but our employer found me. He has helped to continue my research privately, and only now can I control this strange stone completely.' The Doctor pointed. 'Like your bullhook, Mr Hayter, I only have to hurt them a little and then remind them of the pain to get them to do my bidding. Perhaps you should try a stone.'

Hayter gasped. 'I'm not losing an eye for one of those!'

'No, no,' the Doctor assured him. 'Set it in your hook; channel your thoughts through it.'

Hayter became mesmerised with the concept that he too could attain the Doctor's powerful skills. 'How do I get a stone?' he asked.

The Doctor smiled. 'Ask the Viscount – he has a whole collection of them.'

'The Viscount?' Hayter said, astonished.

'Indeed. Our employer is very much interested in how and why these stones work. He has been for a long time. He is now also very interested in that saur boy who took your tyrant. He must have a stone set in something like a necklace to be able to control them.'

Hayter shook his head. 'Nope. Like I said, he was feral – raised by Shadow Raptors from a baby – all he wore were feathers.'

'Surely not, that's impossible,' the Doctor said. 'They are not nice creatures; he would never have survived.'

'I was there with the Viscount when his parents died and he was taken, and there, eleven years later, under the same damn tree when he returned,' Hayter spat. 'That saur boy, his sister and his whole damn family have turned my life upside down. And, worst of all, he took my tyrant.' Hayter gritted his teeth. 'Unlike us, that boy doesn't use fear to tame the saurs. I've seen it. He looks at them with loving eyes, hypnotises them with kindness, and they all do what he wants, just like that,' Hayter said.

'I would like to meet this boy and see this for myself one day,' the Doctor mused, tapping his chin.

Hayter remembered why he'd come to see the Doctor in the first place. 'So what's the story with the night killings? What's all that in aid of?'

'Well, Mr Hayter,' the Doctor replied, stroking his upper lip with a long finger, 'there are several reasons. Right now we're looking for the perfect breed of tritops for a new way of mass farming, tritops that I can help bring to maturity quicker and to market faster than other saurs, not the everyday farmed ones. I'm also looking into the biological properties of certain glands only found in pure breed or wild saurs that are not present in domesticated saurs. I need to shop around and run experiments until I find everything I need.'

He paused, and then continued. 'The tyrants are also part of my study. I'm feeding them my own enriched glandular extracts to advance them in ways never seen before. One day soon I hope to bring these advantages this to humans. That is why the Viscount has bought this train – so we can move about and take what we want unnoticed. It's so much more efficient than a permanent residence, and we have a lot of ground to cover.'

The Doctor put an arm over Hayter's shoulder and started walking to the end of the carriage. 'Now, I don't know about you, but I'm starving, and like to eat the finest and freshest tritop steak for breakfast. Would you care to join me?'

24

The Trek Home

~ the life you should be living ~

'The Great Zino has not been seen here for many years,' Wolf said as they rode along. 'The white man came in long wagon trains with bullets that took them away from the earth. Like the Great Apatosaurs, they were all gone in a few short years.

'The zino is an omnivore,' Wolf continued. 'Its claws may be the longest of all creatures, but they're for tearing apart termite mounds and getting to the soft grubs inside. They also use them to dig out burrows to wait out the cold winters, and then lay eggs in them. But the settlers feared them.'

'Whatever's been mutilating the tritops and cattle must have had a go at this poor creature,' noted Cash. 'Thankfully their claws are also for protection.'

They rode on for a while before Cash picked up the conversation again. 'Wolf, you know the land better than me – have you ever seen others zinos about?'

'I was hoping you would not ask me that question,' Wolf replied.

'Why?'

'If I said yes, would you go looking for them?' Wolf asked warily.

Cash nodded. 'But only to make sure they were protected.'

'Would you tell others?' asked Wolf.

Cash nodded again. 'A select few to help me protect them.'

Wolf raised his eyebrows. 'What if I was already one of those people?'

Cash thought for a moment. 'Then I would have to earn your trust before you told me.'

Wolf smiled. 'You and the boy understand things a lot better than most of your people. Why do you think I took you to the mineshaft?'

'To find the red water,' Cash replied.

Wolf looked more deeply at Cash. 'Is that all you found?'

'No – Carter found the zino as well,' he said.

Wolf nodded. 'We are meant to do the things we do for a reason. There is always a greater cause. The bear was meant to scare you; I was meant to save you. We were meant to camp next to the Saurmen on the wall, and Carter was meant to find the Great Zino.'

Cash nodded firmly. 'And I was supposed to ask you the question about other zinos.'

Wolf smiled back with his wise eyes. 'I think we're

gong to get along, my friend. I will answer your question in good time.'

♦ ♦ ♦

The journey was steady, but slow. The old wagon was heavy, and at several points they all had to dismount to help manoeuvre it round difficult rocky sections to get to the lower plains. The evening had drawn in around them but they kept on, until darkness and a close encounter with an unseen ravine forced them to stop.

'We'll move off at dawn. It won't be long before we're safely back to the ranch, so I'll take first watch,' Cash announced, but Wolf waved him away. 'Matti wants a cuddle and his pine nuts; he's lingering back and waiting for you all to rest. Let me take the whole night's watch and then sleep in the cart tomorrow.'

Cash wanted to refuse, but out in the darkness Matti let out a low roar that confirmed Wolf's assessment of the situation.

As the zino had all the blankets, Cash stoked the fire high and saw that Carter had tucked in close to Buster and snuggled into his black feathers. Cash glanced at Looper, who stared warily at the bear, and tugged him closer to the fire, before tucking himself under the allo's forelimbs, and, taking a lesson from his nephew, slept close to his saur.

Matti was happier to not have an allosaur staring at him and turned a few times to find the right spot to settle, knowing Wolf was watching over them all.

◆ ◆ ◆

Theodore woke up freezing. The fire had died out and the early-morning chill was extraordinarily cold down in the curved canyon. He looked around and noticed that Lambert must have swiped his blankets in the night, as he was huddled under them fast asleep. It was still dark in the saur graveyard, as the sun had not yet filled this thin cut in the earth's surface. Theodore looked up to the sky, where some stars, still faintly visible, were being extinguished one by one by the new day.

Suddenly a dot burned brightly at the top of the canyon just past where the twins slept eternally in their carved temple. The light grew outwards, then rapidly stretched sideways, so that it now reached all along the top. It then slowly started to slip down into the canyon. As the sun rose, it caught a single rock, before widening and illuminating the steep walls. As Theodore gazed at it, he noticed that the rock that had first caught the sun was more like a carved indentation in the wall. Next to it on either side was a similar indentation. These notches all ran along the perimeter of the canyon's walls, but as they ran in a curve they all had a slightly different amount of light and shade. Together they looked like the seconds marked out on a clock's face, evenly distributed and proportioned.

Theodore realised that every morning the sun rose in a slightly different position and hit the indentation next to the one before. The Saurmen who found this strange canyon and carved the temple knew about astronomy, and had turned this place into a giant calendar.

Lambert slept on while Theodore took the opportunity to get another look at some of the inscriptions and drawings that adorned the walls. When he and Franklin had first found this place they had spent a good few days drawing everything in detail and taking notes. These formed the earliest of Franklin's journals. But as Theodore gazed closely at the canyon in the morning light he realised that there was much more to be learnt here. He'd have to return and conduct a much closer investigation. Now that he knew he could trust his saur to find the way, he was confident he'd be able to find it again. If a cold man hadn't taken all the covers, Theodore might have slept on and missed the dawn strike a rock, causing him to notice one more amazing thing about the Saurmen. Everything happens for a reason.

◆ ◆ ◆

The train had rocked Violet and May to sleep as it wound its way back to Sacramento. Bea had been staring out of the window for an hour before Anya, who was sitting opposite, spoke.

'Well, my dear? Did you enjoy our trip?' she asked.

'Yes,' admitted Bea. 'It was one of the most memorable trips of my life!'

'And there could be many more,' said Anya, smiling.

'More film premieres?' said Bea with curiosity.

'Not just film premieres,' Anya replied, leaning forward. 'Opera. Theatre. Grand dances and the ballet.

Visits to the greatest houses of Europe. Mixing with kings and queens. The aristocracy.'

Bea shook her head. 'Somehow, I don't think that's me,' she said.

'But it is,' urged Anya. 'You fit perfectly into this way of life, because it's the way of life that is meant for you. This is the life you should be living, Beatrice. Not like an animal in jungles, wearing clothes that a . . . a ranch hand might wear. You are a young lady, Beatrice, a young lady of substance, and you deserve better than the life you've had of late. And the Viscount and I can give you that.'

Bea regarded her, puzzled. 'Lambert?'

'He is your brother's godfather, Beatrice. You are an orphan, let me remind you. The Viscount can be a real father to you. We can be your parents – look after you, give you the lifestyle you deserve.'

Bea looked at her, bewildered. 'But I feel comfortable in working clothes and riding saurs,' she protested.

'You can still ride saurs,' said Anya. 'Many young women do – but properly, not roughly, like a worker. Because you are not a worker, Beatrice. You will soon no longer be a child, but a young woman. You deserve the best that life has to offer. And the Viscount and I can give it to you.' She leant forward further as she added quietly, 'And we are family. To you and your brother.'

'But . . . what about Theodore?' asked Bea, concerned.

Anya shrugged. 'Who is Theodore, really? He was a

child of the streets who was taken in by your grandmother and grandfather out of the goodness of their hearts, I am told. He's had a pleasant life at their expense, but essentially he's a servant. He's not family.'

'He is to me,' insisted Bea, anger rising in her voice.

Anya shook her head. 'Your father named Lamprecht as your brother's godfather, not Mr Logan,' she said. 'He told my husband that he was fully intending to extend that same honour to you, but sadly he died before he could formalise the arrangement. So, you see, it is the Viscount, and not Mr Logan, who is the real family to you and your brother, as chosen by your father. And, as the Viscount's wife, I would be proud to be part of that same family.'

'But, Theodore –' spluttered Bea helplessly.

'Theodore is the one who kept your father's precious journal from you,' cut in Anya. 'He decided to keep it for himself, against your father's wishes. Lamprecht brought it to America to give it to you because he cares for you and he knew that it was what your father would have wanted –' she paused – 'to continue his research.' She examined her perfectly manicured fingernails while she let this sink in. She went on once Bea's shoulders had sunk almost imperceptibly. 'What is Mr Logan's real purpose? He insinuated himself into your family many years ago, and has stayed there ever since, living off them. We don't need to live off you, Beatrice. Money is no object for us. We can offer you everything your heart desires.'

25

Acclimatised to Freedom

~ change of plan ~

Bonnie heard the sound of the allosaur skidding to a halt outside, followed by the clatter of boots on the porch, and then Cash burst into the house, breathless.

'Where is everyone?' he gasped. 'Aren't they back yet?'

'No,' said Bonnie, getting up. 'What's the matter?'

'We found a Great Zino up in the red hills.'

'A zino!' exclaimed Bonnie.

'She's wounded, and about to lay eggs,' said Cash.

Bonnie was stunned.

'Carter's with it and a man we met named Wolf. They're a few hours back, moving her slowly on an old mining cart. I rode ahead to pick up the truck and get some ranch hands to clear a space for her in the old barn.'

Bonnie grabbed his arm as he was about to run off.

'We had visitors prowling about while you were away, Cash,' she said ominously.

'Are all the saurs okay?'

'Yes,' she said quickly. 'They were looking for you, and the tyrant.'

Cash nodded. 'Let me deal with that later,' he said, as he gave her a squeeze and headed back outside, leaving the screen door to swing wildly on its hinge and then smack shut.

◆ ◆ ◆

Theodore and Lambert were about a mile from the Kingsley ranch when they spotted Cash's truck with Carter, Buster and another man riding alongside.

'Something's wrong,' said Theodore, suddenly alert.

'How can you tell?' asked Lambert.

'Look how fast they're moving.'

Theodore urged his allosaur into a gallop, with Lambert chasing after him. As they drew near, Theodore could see it was a large feathered saur of some sort on the wagon, but couldn't make out what kind it was. Carter waved for them to come up close.

'Trouble?' called Theodore.

Carter gestured into the back of the truck. 'I found her in an old mineshaft.'

Theodore let out a whistle of amazement.

'Is that a Great Zino?!' he exclaimed. 'I didn't know there were any left!'

'If this one doesn't make it, there won't be,' said Wolf.

'This is my new friend, Wolf,' said Carter.

'I'm Theodore, and this is Lambert.' They all nodded to one another.

'I'm going ahead to get a nest ready for her,' said Carter, and he and Buster headed off at a gallop towards the ranch.

'A Great Zino?' remarked Lambert, astonished. 'What's wrong with it?'

'Something attacked her,' said Wolf.

'How badly is she hurt?' Theodore asked.

'Very bad,' Wolf answered. 'And she's about to lay eggs,' he added.

'Well, this is a surprise,' said Lambert with great curiosity.

On arrival at the ranch, Cash, Theodore, Lambert and Wolf all helped carry the barely conscious zino as gently as they could from the truck to the nest that Carter had prepared, and laid the wounded creature down. Bonnie looked at the injured animal apprehensively.

'Will she live?' she asked, her voice heavy with concern.

Wolf knelt by the zino, his ear close to her beak.

'Is she breathing?' asked Cash.

'It keeps stopping and starting,' said Wolf. He looked at the blood that had crusted over the animal's body. 'At least the scabbing has stopped her bleeding.'

'What attacked it?' asked Lambert.

'Something that doesn't know how rare she is,' grunted Theodore.

Carter leant over and gently patted the feathers down around the zino's face. 'She needs to rest and gather strength,' he said softly. 'She knows she's safe now.'

✦ ✦ ✦

The Pickwick coach sent up a dust cloud behind it that Carter saw from a mile away. He had been sitting in his favourite tree close to the zino's barn for a couple of hours, waiting to be reunited with his sister while Theodore, Lambert and Cash all exchanged stories with Bonnie. As the coach drew closer he felt that there was something different about it, and then he heard something that made all his senses come alive at once – raptors! He leapt down and ran alongside as it came up the long driveway with Bea, Violet and May waving from the windows. Oddly Anya was in the front with the driver. As soon as it pulled up by the water tank, Bea burst forth and embraced Carter. 'We have a surprise for you!' she blurted excitedly.

But Carter already knew what it was. The Pickwick coach was crammed full of exotic Raptors of Paradise and he couldn't wait to meet them all. Before anyone could stop him, Carter had opened the nearest cage to let the imprisoned raptor out. Bea and the twins gleefully followed suit, and soon there were raptors on every seat and surface.

'Darling, how was the shopping?' asked Lambert, who had opened the door for his wife. Anya stepped out and handed him a newspaper with an archly cocked brow.

'My word, you have been busy,' he uttered, as he glanced over the article. 'And this explains why my wonderful new coach is . . . full of smelly raptors.' He forced a weak smile. 'Did you manage to talk to Beatrice?'

he asked his wife quietly.

Anya stepped into the shade, and away from everyone's prying eyes. 'Yes,' she murmured. 'This –' she swept her hand towards the cages being unloaded – 'helped.'

The Viscount nodded. 'Good.'

'And your trip, did you take what you wanted?' she asked primly.

'No,' he said shortly, 'but I learnt much. We need to get back to the train, see the Doctor, and our . . . assistants, and check on their progress.'

Inside the coach, Cash was concerned. 'The timing could not be worse,' he pointed out to Violet and May, who were excited about having so many new colourful pets to look after. 'They all look dehydrated, and we hardly have any water for ourselves, let alone these thirsty raptors.'

However there was little to be done about it except to try their best to accommodate them. Cash had some ranch hands clear one of the smaller barns to use as a halfway house for the raptors to become acclimatised to freedom. It would also keep them safe from whatever was mutilating saurs, and from the distrustful eyes of neighbouring ranchers.

◆ ◆ ◆

After Lambert and Anya learnt that the taps inside the ranch were not working, and that the water available was not only communal but came from an old barrel, they decided that a hotel was in order.

'Bonnie, Cash,' Lambert declared as graciously as he could manage, 'your hospitality has been wonderful, but we have to move on now – business calls, and I fear my wife has had too much excitement.'

'Yes,' Bonnie quipped, 'I thought I saw her crack a smile earlier.'

As Lambert made his goodbyes, Anya had a moment with the girls to say how much the trip had meant to her. When she leant in for a stiff hug, Bea silently wondered how old the Viscount's wife might be. She appeared ageless, her skin so tight and pristine – yet it seemed like it was stretched over old bones.

Carter was still unsure about the correct etiquette one used when greeting or bidding farewell to people. He often overdid it with strangers and appeared rude to friends. This time, however, he got it right: a solid handshake, then a warm hug to his godfather and godmother. Everyone gathered to wave them off, and giggled when Anya squeezed in next to the driver, leaving Lambert to ride in the back of the coach that still smelt strongly of soiled caged saurs.

+ + +

With the zino resting in a dark corner of the other barn, Carter took it upon himself to take each raptor from its cage and comfort it. He sensitively inspected them, and with dignity showed them all that at least some humans were capable of caring. There were forty-four raptors in all, and May promised she would get a book from the town library to identify them all. Carter recognised some, but knew no name to call them by. Some of the Raptors of Paradise must have originated from Papua, or one of the other smaller islands nearly.

'If they survive, they'll make a great addition to the place,' Bonnie said optimistically.

'They're going to need water,' Cash observed gravely. 'We have to go back to the Red Hills,' he explained to Theodore, 'and quick.'

♦ ♦ ♦

The Pickwick coach pulled alongside the long black train, where a large carriage towards the rear had its side door open and ramp leading up to it. Ash and Bishop guided the Pickwick carefully into the train's specially built cargo space. Once parked, Anya and the Viscount stepped out, back into the luxury of their private train.

Anya sniffed. 'Darling, I'm going straight to our carriage. I must destroy these old clothes as soon as possible.' As his wife walked away, the Viscount turned his attention to Ash and Bishop.

'You two, secure this and help the driver clean it,' he barked. 'And where are the Doctor and Hayter?'

The two men pointed to the back of the train.

♦ ♦ ♦

The Viscount opened the door into the Doctor's laboratory.

'Change of plan,' he snapped. 'Logan turns out to

know more than I thought, but he wasn't giving much away.' He stamped his foot in exasperation. 'He also has his own keystone.'

The Doctor looked blankly at him. 'Does he now . . . ?' he drawled.

'His delusions of being a true Saurman are yet to be confirmed, but his stone certainly works for finding temples. You would have loved the place.'

'Temples are not my thing, Viscount,' the Doctor said, putting his instruments down.

'This one was a mass saur graveyard.'

'Now I'm interested,' the Doctor said. 'And the twins, who were they?'

'Older than I imagined,' the Viscount replied. 'Ancient. They outdate the natives and are curiously joined at the hips.'

The Doctor only ever gave away mere glimmers of emotion or expression, and at this news the Viscount could see the muscles around his eye twitch behind his darkened glasses.

'And you have the other stone?' the Doctor asked.

'Logan wants it for Carter, the boy with unusual skills I told you about. His reasons made a lot of sense. Could be worth waiting to see if his theory is correct. I'll have to take it from the boy another time. There's no rush to see what happens when I reconnect both halves,' he said.

'So you don't want Logan dead?'

'Sadly we need to keep them all alive,' the Viscount replied. 'Hang back and observe for a while. I had my opportunities to get rid of Logan, but he might be useful for the time being. The girl might need more persuasion as well,' he added. 'She and Anya bonded, but not in the way I planned. I have also read that Mr Chang's West Coast Trading has ceased business.' He slammed the newspaper onto the table. 'But we can't get distracted by that – we have a more pressing issue. A very rare saur has been found, and it's at the Kingsley ranch. The boy Carter somehow befriended it.'

'What is it?' the Doctor asked, full of curiosity.

'A Great Zino,' the Viscount replied, licking his lips.

The Doctor, who was already standing still, stopped moving altogether. 'But they are extinct,' he stated flatly in disbelief.

'Not this one,' the Viscount told him. 'This one is right on the cusp – it's been bitten, probably by your stray tyrant.'

'Where was this?'

'Close to the old mines where the water has been blocked,' the Viscount elaborated.

'Clever – it's making its way back to the pack,' the Doctor said admiringly.

The Viscount paused, and with a more serious tone said, 'Is that where you're hiding them?'

'Yes, in the old shafts beside the haunted town,' the Doctor replied smugly. 'No one goes there; it's the perfect place.' He reached for his jacket. 'I'll need to take the train to get a head start,' he declared.

'You'd better,' the Viscount warned him, 'or there'll be hell to pay.'

'But the zino,' added the Doctor, 'I need to experiment on it – it's an opportunity we can't afford to miss.'

The Viscount ignored him. 'How is Mr Hayter behaving?' he asked instead.

The Doctor considered this. 'Very well,' he answered. 'He could be more effective with his own keystone, though. I could train him.'

The Viscount nodded. 'I will send him to retrieve the Great Zino.'

The Doctor clicked his heels, and gave a short bow.

26

A Carnival of Deadly Creatures

~ safe on my property ~

Two trucks turned off the path and drove up the driveway to the Kingsley ranch. They stopped short of the house and from them disembarked a large group of angry-looking ranchers.

'Let me come with you,' said Theodore to Cash.

'No – you stay back with the children; I'll deal with this,' said Cash, as he walked up the middle of the drive and stood to greet them with a firm expression.

'Afternoon,' Cash said coldly as they approached. 'I can't remember inviting you all – what's your business?'

Cody made his way to the front of the crowd and spoke up. 'That tyrant of yours, where you keeping it?'

'Safe,' replied Cash.

'Safe where?'

'Safe on my property.' Cash shifted his weight and crossed his arms.

Someone in the crowd shouted out, 'Liar!'

'Where you been the past few days?' accused Cody.

'That's none of your business, my friend,' Cash replied.

'It became my business when I lost my best breeding tritops last night,' Cody snapped.

'I'm sorry to hear that,' Cash said less aggressively, genuinely concerned.

'Some folks came a few days back to ask you the same question, but you weren't around,' Cody said. 'They took the precaution of checking on the tyrant, but it wasn't here either.'

'Sounds a lot like trespassing to me,' Cash warned.

Cody shook his head. 'Just paying a visit, that's all. Then some of us found tyrant tracks, out on our property, alongside some dead saurs. You can see how this looks.'

'I have a badly injured saur here as well,' Cash told him. 'I found it in the hills. Probably attacked by the same thing – but not the black tyrant. That was with me the whole time.'

'All of us have lost livestock; some've had multiple deaths – others, single attacks. All ripped apart by something that fits a tyrant's claw and teeth marks – and now we have tracks to prove it.' Cody swept his arms around him to indicate the scale of the problem. 'Now, ask anyone you like if they've seen any tyrants here in the past fifty years and they'll all say just one: a black tyrant upsetting proceedings at a county fair paraded around by your family, Cash Kingsley.'

'I'm telling you, Buster had nothing to do with it,' Cash retorted. 'These attacks started happening before he even arrived!'

'We have no proof of when that tyrant arrived here!' Cody exclaimed. 'It has to die. We can't afford to lose any more livestock. Hell, if it ain't bad enough, all our water's turned red – and you know what that means.'

Cash let out an involuntary laugh. 'You can't be serious?'

'I guess Peabody's curse had some teeth after all,' Cody said.

'I know the real reason why the water's turned red,' Cash shouted, 'and it's got nothing to do with Old Man Peabody, but a lot to do with the old mines.'

'Go on,' barked Cody.

'I rode up into the Red Hills searching for the source of the water a few days ago,' Cash explained. 'And I took the black tyrant with me. I found an old deserted mine filled with red water.'

'That's because of Old Man Peabody, I'm tellin' you,' Cody reiterated.

'No, it isn't,' Cash insisted, his jaw set. 'It's because the old mines are filled with the same minerals that make all these hills red. It's finally seeped into the source and turned it red.'

'How's that going to help us?' Cody spat. The crowd was getting restless.

'Look,' Cash called out, 'we're desperate as well. It'll

take me another day to head back out there, and another few after that to find out how to remedy the situation – assuming it can be fixed. We should all be working together, rather than fighting about it.'

His words hung in the dusty air.

Suddenly a ghastly screech rang out across the yard from one of the barns.

'What's that terrible noise?' demanded Cody, spooked.

Cash sighed. 'It's the saur I found half dead in the hills,' he admitted. 'She's having trouble laying eggs, and can't be disturbed.'

'Nothing I know makes a noise like that,' Cody protested. 'What is it?'

'Just a wild saur,' Cash said calmly. 'Look – she's upset, in pain, and laying eggs. Give her a break.'

But Cody's patience had run out. 'I warned you, Cash Kingsley,' he growled. 'Now you have to be straight with me. Is it a female tyrant laying eggs? I asked if you were breeding them some days back, remember – now prove you ain't lying to me.'

'Fine,' Cash conceded. 'But just you.' Cash shot warning glances at the crowd to let them know he meant it, and stomped off, with Cody close behind.

'No sudden movements,' Cash warned as they entered the barn softly, and made their way round some large equipment to the back, where Carter was keeping watch over the makeshift nest.

'She's laying, stay back,' he whispered.

The zino wasn't happy at the intrusion and tried to stand tall in defence.

'What on God's earth is that?' exclaimed Cody under his breath.

'She's probably the last of her kind – a Great Zino,' Cash replied.

'A great what?' Cody said. 'I ain't ever seen one of those – it's huge!'

The zino nervously tried to swoosh them away.

'Whoa, look at those claws!' Cody exclaimed, ducking out of the way and beating a fast retreat to the safety of the back wall. 'I asked you straight up if you had any other dangerous saurs, and you lied.'

'She's not dangerous,' Cash explained. 'She's an omnivore.'

'I don't care what it eats – those claws are monstrous!' Cody said. 'Now I can see why the tritops were slashed to bits. There's been more than a tyrant feasting on my livestock!' he cried in alarm. 'That's why we've got multiple kills!'

Cash rolled his eyes in exasperation. Everything was backfiring, but the worst was yet to come. Cody unlatched the barn door in an attempt to flee, and immediately stepped back outside to face Matti the bear, who reared up high on his back legs and let out a bone-tingling roar.

'Quick!' Cody shouted. 'Get a gun!'

'It's only Matti.' Carter hushed him, a finger to his lips. 'He's probably looking for Wolf.'

'What!?' Cody yelped. 'You got a wolf here as well? Boy, oh boy, Cash, that's the last nail in your coffin. Next you'll be telling me you have another barn full of raptors!'

Carter nodded happily.

'That's a joke, right?' Cody said in alarm.

Cash sighed. 'You might as well know everything – I have nothing to hide.'

Cody was furious. 'And what's the excuse you've cooked up for keeping those – that they're pets?'

Cash bit his lip. 'Kind of,' he said uneasily. 'My daughters and niece acquired them through a pet shop in San Francisco yesterday.'

'And you expect me to believe all this?' Cody spat incredulously.

'You obviously don't read the newspapers,' replied Cash.

Cody looked at him. 'What's that got to do with anything?'

Carter and Cash exchanged a look.

'So let me get this straight,' Cody said. 'It turns out you have on this ranch a black tyrant, the last Great Zino, the biggest bear in the world, a wolf and a barn full of raptors. Cash Kingsley, this is far worse than a spooky old curse – it's a carnival of deadly creatures!'

'Wolf is actually a person; he was named after his

parents . . .' Cash shrugged, knowing it was not going to do much good.

Without warning, there came a low and loud buzzing noise that grew louder as it passed overhead, lightly shaking the wooden barn as it went.

Carter opened the door to see a startled Matti being led away by Wolf, while the girls and Theodore looked to the sky, where a light aircraft buzzed past them again.

'Is that Micki?' asked Theodore, squinting to get a better look.

Bea spoke up apologetically. 'Theo, I forgot to mention, what with all the commotion, that we might have some visitors arriving – and you needed to clear a runway for them . . .'

'There's no time for that now,' Theodore shouted, 'it looks like Micki's trying to land on the driveway!'

The shocked mob of ranchers all made a break for the relative safety of a stand of trees.

'What on earth?' yelled an astonished Cash.

'That's just Micki Myers and Monty Lomax popping in to say hello,' Theodore explained with a grin.

'The actor?' Cody said, still shell-shocked from discovering the extent to which problematic creatures had become a fixture of his friend's ranch. Now, it seemed, he had to cope with the unlikely appearance of his favourite action hero dropping out of the sky as well.

'He's a friend of ours,' Bea replied breezily.

Theodore, meanwhile, had hatched a plan. 'Cash, we could hitch a ride over to the Red Hills, and try to spot where the water is. We could cover huge areas in no time at all.'

The plane made one last circuit before coming in low, and dipped its wings left, then right, to level out. A line of saplings waved frantically as the plane shot past them. Further up towards the ranch, more mature trees lined the driveway where the angry mob were cowering as far out of the way as possible. There was so little space on either side of the plane's wings that if it had swerved even a little, it could have easily clipped them. The engines roared as it shot by, trying to slow down as quickly as possible.

'They're running out of runway!' shouted Violet.

'And heading for the water tank!' yelled May.

Micki confidently guided her new plane round the tank and rolled gently to a stop, much to everyone's relief.

The side door flapped open and Monty stepped out, waving at the group assembled, their mouths agape. 'Surprise!' he said brightly, throwing his arms out wide.

27

The Ghost Town

~ his curiosity overflowed ~

The astonishing arrival of Monty and Micki made the mob more agreeable. The movie star introduced himself, signed a few autographs, and Bea even took a group photo of them all together, promising to get it duplicated. Cody, still dubious that Cash was up to something, finally left with a warning.

'Get the water flowing again,' he told Cash, 'and we might all take a different view on the dangerous saurs you're keeping here.'

Theodore was delighted to see his old friends Monty and Micki again, as he was sorry to have missed them in San Francisco, and made sure Cash and Bonnie were properly introduced. Bonnie was all aflutter having such important guests, especially as they'd been thoughtful enough to bring with them a huge box of chocolates and a barrel of fresh water.

Once the dust had settled, and with Wolf and Carter's help, the Great Zino laid a clutch of eight eggs and rested over them. Wolf applied some honey to her wounds while the others made arrangements for an aerial expedition over the Red Hills.

It was decided that Theodore, Bea and Carter would go with Micki to conduct a reconnaissance flight to search for the source of the problem while Cash remained behind to prepare the wells for water once it came through. Cash showed Micki where to look on the map. Violet and May, meanwhile, relished the opportunity to show Monty around the ranch and give him a display of their trick-riding skills. Their turn in Micki's fancy new aeroplane would come later.

Micki got everyone to help sweep loose stones from the drive, and after a bone-rattling take-off they were airborne. Carter was silent. This was his first time in a small plane and quickly the tallest tree was well below them. Cash and the girls were now dots on the driveway, and the huge apatos in their paddock were like small lizards. The Red Hills, a day's ride away and usually just a distant haze on the horizon, quickly grew bigger as the plane flew higher over the landscape. A long snake-like black train belched out steam below as they flew on.

As the plane approached the old mining town, they could pick out the trails that used to serve it winding through the rocks.

'Look, water!' exclaimed Bea, pointing out of her window, where a large lake sparkled in the sunlight.

'And over there,' Carter pointed out.

From the plane, many lakes, rivers and waterways were visible, proving that the water hadn't disappeared at all, but must have been diverted. Micki circled around and made a low sweep to get a better look. The largest body of water was nestled just above and behind the old mining town in a natural basin.

'That's not on my map,' Micki remarked, handing it over to Theodore.

'Can you land so we can take a closer look?' he asked.

'I'm going to have to land further down where it's less rocky,' Micki replied. She looped around and spotted a dried-up lakebed that was just long enough for a landing.

'I think we might have found the source of the problem,' Theodore said. 'That lake should be fed from the stream that's blocked.'

Micki touched down with just enough room to bring the plane to a skidding halt, scaring some tritops who'd come looking for a drink.

'We can trek on foot up to the old town from here,' declared Theodore, as he climbed out, 'and find out what's blocking the stream.'

'I'll stay with the plane and prepare a runway to take off from,' Micki told them. 'If you need my help, just use these.' She handed Theodore and Bea some emergency signal flares.

The ghost town sure lived up to its name, and Bea felt a shiver run down her spine as she walked past an old

graveyard. Most of the buildings and half-broken wooden structures had been bleached a pale grey from the harsh winters and hot summers. Any exposed metal had turned to rust as red as the soil. Once-hard surfaces flaked like dry skin as they returned to dust and crumbled into the ground. Scraps of ragged, faintly patterned cloth, which had once been someone's pretty curtains, hung from windowless frames. Bea could just make out the words 'BARBER SHOP' on a wooden sign hung over a doorway, and above it a rusted section of corrugated metal flapped like an old man's hairpiece in the breeze. The only sound was the wind that whistled as it passed over, through and round the buildings.

Carter took a keen interest in an old stagecoach, whose wheels had weeds entwined through the spokes. It was as if the land was rooting it to the spot until it ceased to be useful and just became a pile of wood once more. Theodore saw a sign over one large building that made him smile. He stepped carefully onto the rickety boardwalk that ran in front and along most of the main street and peered in through a broken window. The saloon still had seats round tables, a selection of animal and saur heads stuffed on the wall, and an upright piano in the corner. As he scanned the room, a movement caught his eye, and he was shocked to see a dusty face looking straight back at him from the opposite wall. He froze for a moment, and so did the person staring at him. It was his own reflection in a dusty mirror that had spooked him.

'See any ghosts?' Bea asked, making him jump out of his skin.

'Only one – me,' he replied, and was about to tell her off for sneaking up on him when a chilling howl echoed through the town, carried by the wind. Bea and Theodore stood stock still, their eyes wide.

'I hope that was Carter doing one of his imitations,' Bea whispered nervously, but judging by the look on Carter's face as he turned the corner onto the boardwalk, it wasn't.

'Tyrant,' he said quietly.

'There are no tyrants here any more, Carter,' Bea tried to explain, but then there came a second short barking, then another long howling sound.

'Okay,' Theodore announced, 'I think it's time to head out of town and up to the spring.' The concern was evident in his voice. As he stepped forward, his foot punched through a hole in the wooden floor that sent him tumbling to the ground, and just as quickly up to his feet again in one move.

Bea stepped over the hole and joined Theodore and Carter, jogging quickly away from another long howl that made the hairs on their necks stand upright and their sweat turn cold.

It was not until they had reached the graveyard that Bea noticed Carter was no longer just behind them.

Of course Carter was gone. He was fearless, and instinctively headed towards, rather than away from the strange noises. Bea and Theodore made their way back quickly and found Carter standing in the entrance of an old mineshaft that fed into the rock face on the other side of town. The calls and barks were now amplified by the deep chamber.

Bea grabbed Carter's arm and pulled him to the side. 'We're here to solve the water problem, not discover whatever's making that ghostly sound,' she whispered firmly in her brother's ear.

Carter stayed put. 'Why are there many different tyrants here?' he asked.

Theodore peered round and into the darkness just as a barking noise echoed. 'That does sound a bit like a Ronax,' he said thoughtfully. 'But Bea is right – we could scale up the rocks here to the water.' He pointed upwards. 'Come on Carter,' Theodore urged.

Bea wasn't keen to hang about, and took the initiative to climb up. Theodore began his ascent too, but turned round just in time to see that, instead of following them, Carter was making his way to the source of the strange sounds.

'Damn your curiosity, Carter,' Theodore muttered, gritting his teeth as he dropped back down to the ground.

'What's up?' Bea called.

'You go ahead,' Theodore said. 'I'll get your brother.'

Carter was a good few steps inside the mineshaft, waiting for his eyes to adjust, when Theodore tiptoed in.

'I hear chains,' Carter said. 'Tyrants are chained up like Buster.'

'You sure?' Theodore asked.

'Yes. They don't like the darkness. If they could, the tyrants would come out, so they must be chained up in there.'

'I don't think we should go any further,' Theodore cautioned, 'and I don't have a torch . . . but, hang on, I've got the flares Micki gave me.' He took one out and struck it on a rock, which sent a shower of bright red sparks gushing from the end. He held it up and saw, to his shock, a huddled mass of feathers with the distinctive shape of tyrants' heads facing them. Theodore counted eight sets of eyes glinting in the dark.

'Chained, like I told you,' said Carter, clearly upset.

'How did you get here?' bellowed a voice from behind them, causing Carter and Theodore to jump out of their skins and spin round. Standing half silhouetted against the brightness of the mineshaft entrance, and now partially illuminated by the red flare spluttering in Theodore's hand, was a man dressed all in black, wearing a pair of dark round glasses.

28

The Mouth of the Mineshaft

~ the saloon ~

'You're correct.' The strange man addressed Carter. 'They're chained and perfectly safe to be with.' He paused, turning round. 'However, these other tyrants are not.'

To Theodore's dismay, three more tyrants stepped into the mouth of the mineshaft and stood beside the man. Carter could see these better and studied them closely. Two were brown with shaggy matted feathers around their heads, neck and shoulders. The other was golden-coloured and had unusually long and sturdy forelimbs.

'Who are you?' asked Theodore. 'And why are you hiding tyrants down these mines?'

'You're not in any position to be asking questions,' the man pointed out.

'We were just passing by and heard them,' Theodore replied evenly.

'Where is the girl and how did you get here? I see

no horses, allosaurs or that Black Dwarf Tyrant,' barked the man.

'I'm so sorry,' Theodore said cautiously. 'Please forgive us if we were trespassing. Your accent, is it German?' Then something struck him. 'How do you know we have a Black Dwarf Tyrant?'

The man laughed. 'I saw you all at the county fair. I know perfectly well who *you* are, Mr Logan, and if I am not mistaken that's the Kingsley boy. That is why I ask if you're alone. Normally the girl is with you. Where is she?'

Theodore tried his best to lie. He coughed. 'Back at the ranch,' he said.

The man looked at the ground around him. 'I count three different sets of footprints here. I will ask you again, and if I don't like the reply, I will set my tyrants on you. Where is the girl?'

'You must be mistaken,' Theodore tried. 'Bea stayed behind. Carter and I came up here to find water.'

'Liar!' the man shouted, and the tyrants next to him dipped their heads and took a step closer.

Suddenly a rock fell from above and struck the man on his shoulder. He fell to the ground, cursing in German. Another rock hit the back of the tyrant, making it jump backwards.

'I'm up here, you brute, come and get me!' Bea shouted down.

Theodore sighed deeply as the man rolled over and

looked up to where Bea stood on the edge of a pathway running above the mineshaft. The man turned to the tyrant next to him and lifted his darkened glasses. The reaction was instant. The tyrant looked straight up at Bea and let out a loud series of barks.

'Get her!' the man shouted as the tyrant tried to clamber up the rocks to where she stood.

Carter and Theodore had nowhere to go. Behind them were eight chained tyrants who were now all barking and roaring, and in front stood two more guarding the way out of the mine. The man scrabbled to his feet and clicked his fingers to get the two tyrants' attention. As soon as their heads turned to face the man, Theodore threw his flare at the nearest tyrant, making it step away, knocking the man to the floor with its huge tail. He and Carter ran as fast as they could into the ghost town to take cover.

The man stood back up, cursing under his breath. He clicked his fingers a few more times to get his tyrants' attention away from the red flare that was now spluttering to the end. He raised his darkened glasses and stared coldly into the tyrants' souls.

'Kill them all!' he shouted.

◆ ◆ ◆

Bea peered over the edge again, only to find that to her surprise the tyrant had climbed halfway up the steep cliff. She could see where Carter and Theodore had headed and hoped that the ghost town had good enough places to hide from the two tyrants that were heading their way. The strange man in black had disappeared from view, but she soon realised where. Out from the mineshaft under her came eight more tyrants. They paused for a moment, blinking the daylight into their eyes and adjusting to the day's heat.

Bea figured that heading up was best.

◆ ◆ ◆

Theodore pulled Carter into the side door of the saloon, found his way to the bar, and hid behind it.

'What kind of tyrants are they?' asked Carter quietly.

Theodore waited for a moment, and upon hearing nothing quietly replied. 'The brown ones are just plain old brown ones. The others are Lythronax, Mountain Tyrants.'

Carter looked down. 'They are not friendly.'

'No, they aren't, and neither is their owner,' Theodore said, worried to death about Bea. 'He must be the person behind all the mutilations – Cash thought it was a Mountain Tyrant – but what he's doing it for is a mystery.'

There was a sudden loud crack of wood outside, followed by another. The heavy bulk of a tyrant was on the weak boardwalk and pushing its head through the empty window. As it clipped the top of the frame, part of the wall collapsed, leaving a rectangular collar round its neck that it had to shake off. Theodore and Carter heard it walk away but the ordeal was far from over. A second tyrant sniffed the air, and seeing that there was now a large hole in the side of the building, decided to step inside for a closer sniff.

Theodore saw something move in the corner of his eye and looked up. The same mirror he had seen himself in earlier gave him a good view of the tyrant creeping in with its head low to avoid the ceiling. He then realised their problems had doubled; there was another one behind it. The strange man in black had released the others from the mine.

Theodore tapped Carter on the arm and pointed up to the dusty mirror. Both tyrants were inside now, knocking over chairs and sending up dust clouds as they moved about. One was approaching the bar; the other was by the old piano. Both were sniffing and following trails of scent that would prevent them from remaining hidden for much longer. The tyrant closest to them nudged the front of the bar and snorted. Theodore and Carter were just on the other side. It pushed the bar harder, knocking it back a little, sending an empty bottle to the floor with a smash. This made it jump back, but it became curious enough for a closer inspection. Suddenly the piano tipped over and crashed to the ground. Out from it flew some noisy crows, causing both tyrants to spin round and leap at them, sending dust and furniture flying.

'Now!' Theodore snapped at Carter, as they darted out of the bar, through what had been the old kitchen, and burst outside – only to find themselves right in front of another Brown Tyrant.

Carter swung himself in front of Theodore to face the tyrant. He stared at it with his blue eyes and slowly moved away from Theodore to one side. The tyrant kept staring at Carter, who stepped further away and raised his arms. Theodore could see what the boy was doing; he was luring it away so Theodore could make his escape. Carter knew that the tyrant would not remain calm for long; there was something bigger distracting it. A long low growl echoed past them both, followed by Lythronax barks from the others close by. This was enough to snap the Brown Tyrant out of its temporary placidity. It reached forward and roared with all its might at Carter, who, sensing this was a good time to run, darted over to a chapel, with the tyrant in hot pursuit.

Theodore watched Carter manage to get inside and slam the door in the Brown Tyrant's face. Glancing back to where the mineshaft went into the rock face, Theodore saw three other tyrants above it clambering up a rocky slope, presumably after Bea. Theodore was desperately sorry the children had come along, although there was no way of knowing this was the pickle they'd find themselves in. He was glad Micki was at a safe remove and wondered how long she'd wait before getting help.

Theodore slid to the back of the building and peered round the corner. Down the open road, the man in the black suit and darkened glasses stood looking into the smashed mess of the saloon bar. He had three tyrants with him – which meant there were still another four on the loose.

Then an idea came to Theodore. It might not work, but he had nothing to lose by trying. He waited until the coast was clear and then ran from the building and out of town as fast as his legs could carry him.

29

The Landslide

~ the mass of water ~

Bea was making what she thought was good progress up boulders towards some trees, when the golden-coloured tyrant finally made its way over the edge and onto the pathway where she'd been earlier. Its eyes were trained on her, and seeing that she was close it let out a series of triumphant barks. To Bea's horror there was a reply. More tyrants were barking and bounding over up the pathway towards it. The further up Bea climbed, the tougher it became for her – but not for the tyrants to follow. She glanced back and was relieved to see that one had tumbled down to the pathway, but the other two were still hot on her heels. She took the biggest rock she could lift and tossed it behind her.

'Get back!' she shouted in vain as it missed the closest tyrant by just a few inches. She tried again, managing to strike the second on the shin. It barked out a roar but clambered on. A third rock missed both, so she resumed her climb.

Once she reached the top, Bea found that rather than

levelling out, the ridge dropped steeply down the other side. Running down from this appeared to be what was left of the old stream, which was now only a wet trickle – and, above this, a wall of newly turned rocks was littered with tree debris. Somewhere behind all this must be the new body of water they'd spotted from the plane. She hoped she'd be able to signal Micki from here.

As she scrambled, Bea recalled something Carter had once pointed out to her. Buster had elongated flaps of skin between his arms and body to help him swim, and thick waterproof buoyant feathers to help him float freely. This was because he had needed to traverse the low-lying islands of Indonesia. But the tyrants chasing her were very different; the golden ones had long strong arms that helped them climb over rocks. Perhaps this meant they'd be useless in the water, and she'd finally be able to shake them off?

A boulder Bea stepped on trembled a little, threatening to tip her, so she hopped off just as it gave way. As it fell, it knocked a tyrant all the way down to the bottom. Bea heard a rushing noise and felt her feet get wet. She looked down and noticed that the mass of water the other side of these rocks had found a hole. She turned her attention to dislodging as many as possible. The force of the water flowing out also helped move the small rocks and dirt away from under the larger ones, making these unstable. Bea focused on them, and soon a second and third spout of water rained down onto the tyrants below.

30

The Easy Way,
or the Hard Way

~ two barrels of water ~

Christian Hayter pulled the truck to a halt just short of the driveway leading up to the Kingsley ranch and jumped out. Bishop took his place and drove on with Ash up to the main house.

Hayter crept round the back away from any prying eyes, and up to one of Cash's barns. Ash and Bishop, meanwhile, set into play their distraction, and knocked on the front door. Bonnie answered and kindly accepted the donation of two large barrels of drinking water, which were strapped to the back of the truck. After a short while, Cash came out and helped them unload the heavy barrels.

Hayter saw that the barn door had a padlock on it, which suggested this was the barn the zino was in.

He unclipped his bullhook from his belt, jabbed the end in the padlock, and twisted it until it popped open. The door swung wide and he stepped in.

As he did so, the zino reared up protectively in front of her eggs.

Hayter grinned to himself.

He moved towards the zino, slapping the bullhook against the palm of his other hand. The zino, used to creatures backing off when she displayed, became unsettled by this reaction.

'We can do this the easy way, or the hard way,' smirked Hayter. 'Doesn't bother me.'

Suddenly the zino swung at Hayter with her huge claws. Hayter ducked and let the monstrous talons whistle close just over his head.

'The hard way.' He smiled. 'Okay, if that's how you want it,' he said, and he swung his bullhook, smashing it into the zino's side. The saur let out a high-pitched wail of agony and crashed to the ground. Recovering slightly, she pushed herself up off the dust and reared once more against Hayter, claws extended. Hayter smirked, and unleashed his bullhook again in a vicious swing – but this time the zino jerked back, the hook sliding over her without injury, and, in turn, she let fly with a blow of her own, her claws tearing at Hayter's shirt.

Hayter looked down and saw the splatter of blood grow on his chest where the zino's sharp claws had nicked him.

'Okay, playtime is over!' he snarled angrily. 'Now we get real!'

The Great Zino had retreated, but was still positioned protectively over her eggs, and Hayter knew he had to be careful.

Getting the zino back to the train was important to his employer, and Hayter wanted to keep pleasing him. He saw a rope looped over a hook on the barn wall, made a lasso, and let fly with it, aiming for the zino's head – but the huge creature jerked back, and the lasso made contact only over the zino's wing. She immediately jerked the rope, throwing the man off balance and sending him sprawling.

Hayter hung on tightly as he pushed himself up off the ground, and was just about to pull at the rope when the zino beat him to it, giving a sudden tug. Hayter found himself being pulled towards the enormous creature and the precious eggs. He grabbed at a sturdy pillar with one hand to stop himself from being dragged through the dust and dirt, and then hooked one foot round the pillar too. Using it as a kind of lever to stop the rope, he hauled himself to his feet. Hayter then gave a really sharp pull, catching the saur unawares, and the zino crashed to the ground, narrowly missing the eggs.

'You don't get the better of Christian Hayter,' he spat smugly, but the zino leapt up and hurled itself backwards – and once more Hayter found himself stumbling forward and landing with a thud on the hard ground. Out of the corner of his eye he saw the huge creature rear up, and then its claws smashing down towards him. Just in time, he rolled clear, as the claws ripped into the spot where he had been lying, the sharp talons impaling themselves in the dirt.

As the zino struggled to release her claws, Hayter sprung to his feet and spun the rope over her. As the zino's claws came free from the ground, Hayter ran round her, before pulling tight to close up the slack. This was what Christian Hayter was good at: trussing up saurs for exporting. As the zino tried to work out why she could no longer extend her arms, he whipped the end of the rope round her feet, then pulled fast and hard, bringing the exhausted zino tumbling to the ground.

'Got you!'

Hayter wiped his split lip, spat blood on the dirt, then grinned triumphantly at his handiwork.

From outside, Hayter suddenly heard a noise, and froze. The zino had not gone down quietly, and had obviously attracted some attention. He turned and realised the door was ajar. Ash and Bishop had only one task – keep the owner away by distracting him – but it sounded like they had failed, again. With the zino safely tangled on the floor and unable to stand, he crept up to the door and peered out. There, just a breath away, was the stray Lythronax tyrant that they had been searching for, eyes like fire looking directly at him, mouth wide open, saliva dripping from its razor-sharp teeth.

Hayter stumbled back into the barn, shaking. Without

the Doctor, there was no way to control it. The tyrant cautiously stepped in and paused while waiting for its eyes to adjust to the dim light of the barn before it sniffed the air and confidently stepped further inside. Hayter turned to run, but stumbled and fell over the zino, who let out another weak cry. And then the Lythronax pounced.

Cash peered round the open door of the barn to see what all the commotion was. To his horror, the place was spattered with blood, and standing over the wretched body of the zino was a huge Mountain Tyrant. Cash couldn't believe his eyes; after everything he had gone through to save the zino, it was now torn to pieces – and, worse still, mutilated by a wild tyrant on his ranch. In his horror, he missed the prone body of Hayter lying beneath the zino.

Cash stepped back, hoping not to be seen, and then, when safely outside, ran as fast as he could back up to the ranch.

Ash bumped straight into the running Cash. 'That's both barrels stored,' he said, nervously wiping the sweat from his brow.

Bishop had spied where Cash had run from, and fearing that he had seen Hayter, made a quick excuse. 'We'd better be getting back now.'

Cash was white with fear. 'If I were you, I'd drive as quickly away from here as possible,' he said. 'I'm getting my rifle. There's a tyrant back there that could wipe out everything around us, including my girls!'

✦ ✦ ✦

Hayter came to. He didn't know how long he'd been out and tried to remember how he'd ended up lying on the dirt floor of the barn. His shirt felt sticky, and he saw with shock that he was covered in blood.

He tried to get up, but realised that part of the zino was lying on him. A muffled grunting sound close by made him turn his head, and he saw the Lythronax tyrant's head deep in the dead zino's guts. Suddenly the tyrant stopped chewing on its kill, lifted its blood-covered nose, and looked directly at Hayter. Terror welled up in him as he saw the Lythronax rise up and begin to move towards him, blood and saliva dripping from its jaws.

Then something strange happened. The tyrant froze motionless above him, its eyes rolled back in its mighty head, and it started to gasp for air. Hayter stared in bewilderment. The tyrant's paralysis seemed to come from nowhere.

Just then the barn doors smashed open as Bishop drove the truck into the barn and skidded to a stop just in front of Hayter.

'Jump on, boss!' shouted Ash.

Seizing the moment, Hayter heaved the zino off him, only to find that it was just the head and long neck in one perfect chunk. He looked back up at the tyrant in disbelief; it remained motionless. Somehow he had miraculously been saved. He tossed the head to the side and jumped onto the back of the truck, as Bishop popped it into gear and slammed his foot on the accelerator.

'*Stop!*' commanded Hayter as they lurched backwards.

Bishop slammed on the brakes, jolting them violently forward. 'What is it, boss?'

'I've left something behind!'

◆ ◆ ◆

Cash and Wolf stood in the doorway of the barn, both carrying rifles, dumbfounded at the carnage before them – the remains of the dead zino, her blood and guts spattered all over the inside of the barn.

'I saw it up close –' said Cash desperately – 'it was a Mountain Tyrant.'

'Which way did it go?' asked Wolf, and Cash answered with a nod westwards.

'Who were those men?' Wolf continued.

'I don't know,' Cash replied. 'They said they heard everyone was dry and thought we could do with some water.'

'Looks like you owe them more than two barrels of water.' Wolf bent down to inspect the tyre marks. 'They rammed in here and scared it away,' he added with confidence.

Cash examined the smashed lock. 'Strange that it's been forced open,' he muttered. 'The tyrant couldn't have done that.'

'Is it safe?' asked Monty, peering round the corner

along with Violet and May, now that the coast was clear.

'Yes,' Cash replied, urging them back, 'but you don't want to see this.'

'The eggs, did it eat the eggs?' cried Violet, alarmed.

Cash and Wolf looked at each other as it dawned on them they'd forgotten to check. They stepped over the mess and up to the nesting box Carter had made.

'Looks like they're fine,' said Cash with relief, before adding, 'Hang on – how many were there?'

'Eight,' replied May from the doorway, daring herself to peep in.

'Damn,' cursed Cash. 'One's gone.'

'Let's get them secured somewhere better, as we'll have to incubate them now the mother is dead,' Wolf pointed out.

Cash looked at his new friend. 'To be honest, Wolf,' he admitted sadly, 'we were probably going to have to do that anyway.'

Wolf nodded back. 'Agreed,' he said stoically. 'The zino's wounds were grievous. She would never have made it.'

31

Clash of the Tyrants

~ a darker place ~

The chapel had a back door that led away from the graveyard and to a small footbridge that had once crossed the old river. Carter darted over it, then hid underneath as best he could, hoping the tyrants at the chapel's front door were still trying to get it open. He was frustrated that he couldn't communicate with them to get them to stop. The strange man in black had tapped into a darker place that seemed impossible to charm them away from. Clearly whatever was hidden under his darkened glasses was the source of his power. Carter burned with curiosity to know what it was.

A shadow loomed over the small footbridge – and Carter could see that the tyrant had sniffed him out again. He tossed a handful of rocks and ran out. This delayed the inevitable, but only momentarily. Carter was just setting off when the tyrant pushed him onto the ground. He tried to stand, but was knocked down again – before the full force of the tyrant's foot squashed him down. It pushed with enough force that it squeezed all the air out of him.

Carter struggled to relieve the pressure so that he could breathe. Somehow, he managed to gulp in some air, and tried frantically to wriggle away, but it was useless. He was caught like a mouse in the paws of a cat. The more Carter tried to free himself, the more it pushed down. The tyrant leant in curiously and gave Carter a good sniff before roaring into his face with all its might and displaying its rows of razor-sharp teeth.

'*Stop!*' called the Doctor, freezing the tyrant in an open-mouthed pose. Its eyes looked wildly around until its master slid into view. A huge glob of saliva dribbled onto Carter's chest.

The Doctor tapped his dark glasses, signalling to the tyrant to stand down. It closed its mouth and raised its head back up, but kept Carter pinned underfoot.

The Brown Tyrant's roar brought the others running over. The Doctor turned to face them all and started to raise his dark glasses, but stopped just short of revealing his eye. The tyrants lined up and waited for their next command.

'Now, look what we have found,' the Doctor sneered. 'The raptor boy.'

He walked round to face Carter, who was still struggling under the tyrant's foot.

'I was told you had abilities, yet I see none. Pity, I was hoping to have a bit of fun,' he whined.

Carter tried to say something but there was no way he could with the force of the tyrant bearing down on him.

The Doctor looked around and pointed to the higher ground. 'Your sister won't last long either with three Mountain Lythronax chasing her, and as for that man who is supposed to be looking after you – well, he ran away. Out to the pastures.' The Doctor laughed out loud. 'We let him go, but he won't get far. After eating you, my tyrants will easily pick up his scent and hunt the poor fellow down.'

A few of the tyrants heard something approaching quickly and turned round, alerting their master to a rumbling noise that was coming from behind them. A tremendous wall of dust rose up from a herd of tritops stampeding towards them.

Carter's eyes lit up as he twisted his head and saw, in the midst of the stampede atop the largest tritops, Theodore himself, gripping on to a tritops's neck frill, pointing forward with his knife and shouting, 'CHARGE!'

How on earth? Carter wondered, thrilled to see him. The tyrant holding him saw too, and adjusted his footing.

The Doctor could see that his tyrants eagerly wanted to know what to do. He had trained them not to act until commanded – or he would inflict horrific pain within them.

'Stay,' he shouted, which they all continued to do, but they lowered themselves ready to pounce if the next order came.

The Doctor stepped forward and stood his ground facing the oncoming saurs.

'Been using some Saurman tricks have you, Mr Logan?'
he called out to his oncoming foe. 'At last, something a little
challenging – the boy has been *such* a disappointment.'

He grinned at the tritops bearing down on him and
took off his darkened glasses while laughing to himself.
The black sparkling stone gently flared, and an iridescent
rainbow of colours glistened in the sunlight as he breathed
on the lenses, giving them a little rub with his black-
gloved hands. The Doctor then looked up straight at the
lead tritops, who instantly stopped on the spot, sending
Theodore over its head, through the air and onto the
ground with an almighty thud. Carter looked on with

shock as all of the tritops quickly peeled away and ran just as fast back to wherever it was they had come from. The tremendous noise faded away as the cloud of dust slowly settled back to the ground.

Theodore winced in pain. Something was broken – probably a rib or two – so he dragged himself to his knees and decided to stay there while he got his wind back.

The Doctor laughed. 'Futile attempt, Mr Logan – you have so much to learn from your keystone . . . but sadly you won't live long enough to benefit from any of it.'

The Doctor turned back to Carter, who was still trying to breathe and escape from under the foot of the tyrant. 'As for your pathetic, immature skills, boy –'

He waved over to the seven tyrants patiently standing by his side. 'As you can see, your ability to love saurs may have worked on one weak Black Dwarf Tyrant, but it has no effect on my specially trained berserkas.' He chuckled to himself again. 'I sent that stupid saur of yours into a rage with one little look at the county fair.'

Carter felt something digging into his waist. It was the Shadow Raptor claw he always kept tucked into the belt of his shorts. He managed to inch a hand close and grab it, but with limited movement could do no more than scratch the soft underside of the mighty tyrant's foot.

Surprisingly, this achieved a lot. The Brown Tyrant yelped and recoiled – not in pain, but from the tingling sensation Carter had caused. Suddenly free, Carter scrabbled to his feet with the large sickle claw in hand.

'Now that's more like it!' The Doctor laughed. 'Except that little claw will be just like a thorn prick to my tyrants. You'll have to try much harder than that.'

The Doctor looked to the Brown Tyrant and tapped his eye again. It moved back, lowered its huge head, then roared in Carter's face with such force that it rocked him back on his heels.

But Carter didn't fall. Instead he stared directly into the tyrant's face with a glare of equal intensity, challenging the enormous beast. The tyrant, enraged, raised itself to its full height to tower over Carter, then reached back and breathed in deeply, filling its lungs in order to increase the might in its attack on the boy, driven by pure rage.

Carter copied it and inhaled a lungful of an equally awesome roar. But what came out of his mouth was inaudible to humans. Carter shrilled out a blinding white noise that could be heard by every saur for miles around. Even Buster, chained up out the back of the ranch, heard it. And every saur that heard it was momentarily stunned. The world seemed to pause with anticipation, like a balloon waiting to be popped, or a log under an axe about to fall.

The silence only lasted a few seconds, but to the saurs who were frozen in this moment of paralysis, it felt like an agonising lifetime of emptiness. Theodore stared at Carter in amazement; somehow he was controlling the tyrants around him, making them freeze to the spot with their eyes rolled back as they gulped for air, including the man in black, who grabbed his throat in desperation. Theodore recognised that this was akin to when time had almost stopped for him back at the rodeo, when he made contact with the keystone embedded in his knife's hilt.

When Carter stopped emitting his silent screech, the saurs' vision snapped from bright white back to dark reality. Then came an aftershock, as the balloon popped and the axe struck the log.

The Doctor fell to his knees, and without hesitation scooped his opal keystone eye out from its socket. This immediately released him from the painful echo. He looked round at his stunned tyrants and back to Carter, who swung as hard as he could, and punched the man straight in the face. The opal eye dropped to the floor and rolled towards Carter's feet. He picked it up and looked into it, then at all the tyrants who were standing there, bewildered as to what to do.

The Doctor scrabbled to his feet, shouting, 'Attack him!' but it did nothing.

The crazed man lunged at Carter in a fit of pure rage, but Carter grabbed hold of him and pulled him down to the floor. Carter sprang up quickly as the Doctor clutched at him, but only managed to rip his top. It was a pathetic struggle – not a real fight, as Carter had no intention of harming the man further. He had removed his opal eye, and that was all he needed to do. But, like the saurs that the man in black had controlled, something inside drove the Doctor on relentlessly.

'GIVE ME BACK MY EYE!' he screamed, veins popping on either side of his head.

Then Carter had an idea. He held the opal eyeball out clearly in one hand so that all could see it – then popped it into his other hand, and threw it away over his shoulder.

Theodore, the Doctor and all the tyrants watched it arc through the sky and land some distance behind the

boy. There followed a moment of confusion before the Doctor sprang to his feet, and with the tyrants ran over to where it had landed. Carter waited for the perfect moment, and then darted over to Theodore and pulled him to his feet. With his one good eye the Doctor looked around frantically, before seeing the opal on the ground, and jumped on it.

'Got it!' he yelped with relief, before noticing Carter and Theodore trying to run away. 'Ha! You're not going to get far now,' he cackled. 'I've had enough of your stupid, childish games.' The Doctor spat on the opal eye in his hand to clean it. 'I'm going to show you how it really works,' he growled, clicking his fingers towards the tyrants, who all stood alert.

Suddenly from behind the Doctor, the tremendous rumbling noise returned.

He sighed. 'Oh, please don't tell me you're attempting to try that pathetic trick again. Stupid brainless tritops are no match for my tyrants.'

The Doctor turned round to face not a charging wall of dust and tritops, but water.

32

Broken All Over

~ a glass marble ~

Nothing could have stopped the water once Bea started to release it. As it poured forth, she clung on to the rocks to avoid being swept away. Everything else was caught up in its path: the tyrants, the Doctor, Theodore and Carter. The red water, contaminated with iron that had leached into it, flushed back out into the land.

Theodore had managed to hold on tight to Carter, knowing the boy couldn't swim. They were battered and bruised by rocks, and tossed around like twigs in the raging torrents. Eventually it slowed down enough for them to clamber to the side of the refreshed river. The limp body of a dead tyrant washed past them. Carter could see that Theodore was in a bad way; bleeding from a multitude of cuts, he held his chest and winced in agony.

'The flare!' Carter gasped, pulling it from Theodore's shirt. Luckily the greaseproof paper had protected it from the deluge, and when he struck it on a rock, a glorious shower of red sparkles shot into the air followed by a plume of glowing red smoke.

Carter looked about, and to his relief saw a second column of smoke rising further upstream. This could only mean one thing: Bea was alive. The engines of Micki's plane could be heard overhead as she flew in low, waving at them both. Carter gave a thumbs-up and pointed her towards the second flare. They watched as Micki swooped around and landed beyond some trees to pick up his sister.

Soon enough the plane roared past, and Carter could see Bea up front with Micki waving back. Micki brought it down to land, and a very wet Bea opened the door and ran out to hug her brother.

They both went to help Theodore, who was now surrounded by the same tritops that he had managed to coax into stampeding the tyrants. They were enjoying a refreshing to drink from the refilled river, with Theodore sat limply amongst them.

'Well, we all needed a good bath,' he tried to joke as Bea hugged him. 'Careful – I think I'm broken all over!' He winced in pain as they helped get him into the plane.

From above, everything glistened and sparkled below, as they followed the river all the way back to the Kingsley ranch.

◆ ◆ ◆

Back in his laboratory on board the train, the Doctor took the opalised eyeball from his pocket, put it in a basin of warm water, and washed it carefully so that there was no grit or even a speck of dust on it. He carefully dried the polished sphere, then looked into the mirror above the basin, pulling the flesh back from his empty socket with the fingers of one hand, and was about to insert the eye when he stopped. Something about it didn't feel right. He held it to his good eye, turned it round – and a tidal wave of utter rage surged through his veins. This wasn't his eye! It was just a glass marble! The boy had switched it!

As the Doctor stood in turmoil, looking at his bedraggled reflection, the door flew open. 'Leave me ALONE!' he shouted menacingly.

It was Hayter, covered in blood and dirt. His two henchmen, Ash and Bishop, followed him in, looking exhausted. The men carried a bloodstained sack and a small box.

The Doctor swallowed hard, biting back his bitter disappointment at the loss of his treasured eye.

'I assume there's a reason you burst in without knocking first?' he demanded coldly.

'You bet there is, doc!' fumed Hayter.

A sharp tapping noise from the hallway outside interrupted them.

The Viscount stood there with his cane, looking very displeased indeed. 'I was expecting to feast my eyes on something very special – the last Great Zino.' He spoke sternly. 'Yet, when I went to the livestock carriage to view it, there was no sign of one. In fact, there are no tyrants either.' He regarded the Doctor and Hayter with a cold, venomous look, then noticed something was missing. 'Where's your eye?'

The Doctor, fuming inside, held on to the marble. 'It washed away, and so did all my tyrants,' he spat.

'Explain yourself!' The Viscount stamped his foot.

'Your dam,' the Doctor muttered. 'It broke. Those wretched children were there meddling with it.'

'WHAT? The water's back already?' the Viscount exclaimed. 'But the factory – I haven't purchased it yet!' He leant forward, his hands braced on his knees. 'The

Kingsley children,' the Viscount said in a panic, 'did they see you and the tyrants?'

The Doctor slowly nodded as the Viscount gritted his teeth and turned to Hayter. 'Your task was to bring the Great Zino here. You and this pair of idiots. Where is it?'

'I had the zino. Tethered with rope – a walk in the park, no commotion or fuss. My men did their part; we had it all under control – then, suddenly, the Doctor's missing tyrant turns up. There was nothing I could do to stop it. I'd already tied the zino up – it had no way to defend itself. It was despatched in a moment. I was lucky to walk out alive.'

'It wasn't my fault it escaped,' said the Doctor curtly.

'But you turned it into a killing machine,' Hayter snapped back.

'The Lythronax was already a killing machine,' retorted the Doctor. 'I just increased its potential.'

'And, as a result, the last Great Zino is gone, just like that,' said Hayter accusingly, clicking his fingers.

'My job was to develop the tyrant's natural killing instincts, making them more powerful and more vicious than ever,' said the Doctor. 'I did my job to perfection. It's a pity you and your henchmen didn't do yours, which was to bring the zino back alive.'

'Enough of this petty rivalry!' barked the Viscount. 'I've had my grand hall extended in order to fill it with more hunting trophies, but what heads do I have to mount on the walls?' He looked at them grimly. 'I would mount all your heads if they were perfect examples of the human race, but unfortunately they leave a lot to be desired.'

Hayter smirked. 'We do have one for your walls, sir,' he said, and nodded at Ash, who opened the bloodstained sack he was holding and took out the zino's severed head.

The Viscount's expression warmed, as a small smile replaced his frown.

'It is a start,' he acknowledged.

'It's a shame you couldn't extract its glands first,' grunted the Doctor, annoyed at being upstaged.

'Oh,' Hayter said airily, 'I retrieved those as well.' He pulled out a small sack dripping with blood.

The Viscount nodded with growing appreciation.

'But a live pure-breed Great Zino would have been a lot better to experiment on,' the Doctor spat out in anger.

'Yep, we got one of those too,' said Hayter. He nodded at Bishop, who opened the box he was holding and took out a large egg. 'In a few months you can have your live Great Zino.'

The Viscount's wicked smile spread. 'Very good,' he said, and pondered something for a moment, looking at Hayter with renewed respect.

From his pocket he produced a small pouch, and handed it to his faithful employee. 'And in return, Mr Hayter, this is for you.'

Puzzled, Hayter took the pouch, and studied it. 'Thank you,' he said. 'What is it?'

'Look inside,' the Viscount said. 'It's a gift from me to you for your services, and as compensation for your troubles. This is a gift; I'm giving it of my own free will.'

Hayter felt there was something hard inside, and tipped it out into the palm of his hand.

The Doctor leant in and looked at the object. 'It's a keystone,' he gasped.

The Doctor turned to the Viscount petulantly. 'Why, Herr Viscount, are you not passing this to me? I need to replace my eye. Without it, my research becomes so much harder!'

'I have other keystones, Doctor, fear not. But this one –

this is Mr Hayter's. He has earned it. Now, let's set it in that bullhook of yours, Hayter, and see what it can do. If the missing pages in Franklin's journal are to be believed, it can yield great power in the right hands – even if you're not a Saurman. The secret is in not keeping the power for yourself, but passing it on. It's not something you can buy or take. You just have to connect with it, believe in it – and it will channel your command.' The Viscount smiled to himself. 'I have plenty of other keystones,' he reflected, 'and all but one were either taken or bought.'

'So you don't need this one?' Hayter asked.

Viscount von Lamprecht Knútr didn't reply immediately, but simply smiled at them all. 'Don't you remember, Mr Hayter? You were there in Aru. I was given this one –' he unbuttoned the top of his shirt and pulled on an old leather cord that was round his neck to reveal at its base a strange dark stone that glinted and dazzled sharply in the dim light – 'by that ever so nice chap Franklin Kingsley, just before I shot him.' He squinted as he looked into the stone. 'I bet this was not the destiny he imagined.'

33

The Following Days, Weeks and Months

~ save the saurs ~

In the following days, Cash, with Cody's help, managed to round up five of the surviving tyrants. The bodies of the others were all accounted for and buried – all but the one Cash saw in his barn, that is. Still, no other animals showed up dead, so they assumed it had moved on into the mountains. Figuring that the threat had been sufficiently removed, the apatos were released from the fenced paddock. Carter, finding he could now connect with the formerly deranged tyrants, helped corral them all into the high-sided paddock, where they could recover. Everyone was pleased to see the water flowing once again, including the owner of the closed slaughterhouse. He had been about to sell it all for a dollar to a European rival, but luckily Old Man Peabody's curse had been lifted.

Theodore had a gift for Carter: the twins' keystone – the other half of what his father had wanted him to have. Bea and Theodore had together decided this was the right thing to do, but Carter surprised them both by handing it back to Bea. 'This should be yours,' he said generously. 'One day I will find the one that is rightfully mine.'

In the following weeks, Theodore and Bea read and reread Franklin's last journal and discussed in detail what it could all amount to. It seemed to answer a lot of their questions, but also threw up some new ones. Who were these Saurmen? What was the strange power that the keybones possessed, and how far did their empire stretch? It also gave a better understanding of the last weeks of Franklin and Grace's lives, but failed to mention Lambert. Theodore promised to revisit the mass saur graveyard and introduce Bea and Carter to the twins. There was so much that he and Franklin had missed the first time they found it, and he would need Bea to make detailed notes in a new journal he had bought for her, so that she could continue where her father had left off.

In the following months, and with Wolf's care, the zino eggs hatched successfully. An announcement was made to the press that Great Zinos had made a miraculous comeback. Micki covered the story, and with Monty's patronage, they made plans for the Kingsley ranch to become a sanctuary where the public could view them – as well as some of the most exotic raptors seen outside Indonesia. The 'Save the Saurs' movement was born.

✦ ✦ ✦

Anya Stitz spotted something out of the window of her private carriage as it rolled along. 'Isn't that one of those . . . saurs of yours, darling?' she asked, pointing.

From the observation coach towards the rear of the train Christian Hayter had spotted the same thing. 'Ash, Bishop,' ordered Hayter, 'open the cargo doors!'

The two men slid apart the big doors of the empty livestock carriage.

'Let's see if this stone works,' Hayter said, a slow smile spreading across his face. He held it high into the sunlight and gave a long whistle to catch the Lythronax tyrant's attention as the train whizzed past.

The tyrant saw the sparkling stone and immediately ran at full speed along the side of the train, drew level with the open cargo doors, and leapt in, skidding across the floor and crashing into the wall. It turned towards Hayter, as if it was ready to spring, but instead of jumping at him, it remained crouched, eyes fixed on the stone in Hayter's hand.

Christian Hayter walked over to the tyrant and patted it on the nose. 'Good girl,' he said. 'I think we're going to have a lot of fun – not like with my last pet.'

♦ ♦ ♦

THE END

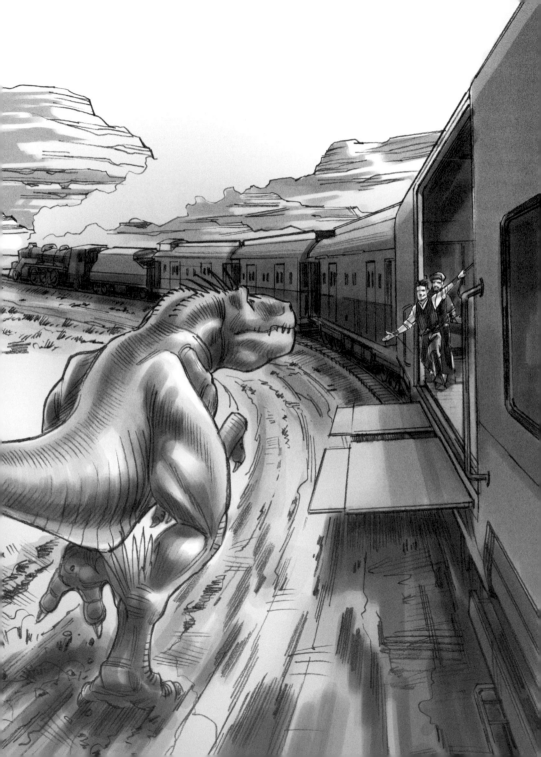

APPENDIX

Excerpts from
Saurs of the Wild

~ by Nigel Winsor ~

Editor's note: Extracts from the updated 2012 edition of *Saurs of the Wild*, with further material by Philip Winsor

CARNOTOR
Carnivore | Biped

These bipedal theropods closely resemble tyrants in shape, with narrow heads with distinctive keratinous brow horns, a short neck, and barrel chests. Their small vestigial forelimbs jut backwards, each with two fused immobile fingers and two single bone-spur fingers. They have long tails, long hindlimbs with three weight-bearing toes, and thick scaly skin. Unlike tyrants, which developed lightweight skin and grew feathers, carnotors' skin grew harder and became armour-like, developing scales and scutes (hard bony external plates) in patches over different parts of their bodies.

Allosaurs and carnotors are the only theropods to have horns made of keratin covering a core of bone, much like impala and other horned mammals. Other horned theropods, such as the Lonesome Horned Tyrant, have horns composed of only bone – these are used predominantly to shade the eye. Male carnotors use their horns in competitive combat, locking together and pushing each other until one yields. Both male and female carnotors also use their horns to scratch and groom themselves, utilising their flexible necks and bodies. Carnators are found on every continent around the world, where they very successfully adapt their appearance to the prevailing environmental conditions.

European Carnotors

Adapted for life hidden in the forests of Europe, the European Carnotor has a short and slender body, tail and neck to manoeuvre

European Carnotaur

stealthily through trees and stalk its prey. Deer and boar can outrun them over long distances, as these carnotors tire quickly, so patience and camouflage are vital to the survival of the species. Some European Carnotors have been known to stand motionless for hours at a time, waiting for their unsuspecting prey to wander past.

Colour variations have developed regionally to reflect the different wooded surroundings of the carnotors' habitats, allowing them to better cloak themselves to their surroundings. Northern European Canators are mostly lightly striped in deep red and brown, reflecting the dense pine forests of Northern Europe. Southern European Carnotors are a paler buff and grey. Typically, in all regional varieties, the female has a pale belly; the male thicker and longer brow horns.

Sightings of European Carnotors are rare and little scientific research has been carried out, so their reputation as demons of the forest lives on. Most regions of Northern Europe have folklore and traditional stories featuring demons living in the forest. Some tales tell of an army who would sneak into a town and devour its inhabitants. The origins of this story may be rooted in the mid-1600s when Grustatter, a remote town in the Black Forest of Germany, was attacked by hungry carnotors. A forest fire had decimated wildlife and much of the carnotor's prey, and surviving animals fleeing the fires had been corralled by hunstmen in Grustatter's town square. The carnotors, driven by hunger, followed their prey and, upon coming into close contact with humans, attacked. Many townspeople did not survive. This story evolved and changed over the years, passed down the generations as a spooky bedtime story, before it was eventually collected and published by The Brothers Grimm.

SAUROPODS
Herbivore | Quadruped

Sauropods were once the longest creatures to walk the Earth. Early fossils show that their antecedents were surprisingly small, but during the time of the dinosaurs sauropods grew to become giants on Earth.

However, after this period, sauropods went through a slow period of phyletic dwarfism (a decrease in average size of animals of a species). Lack of predators or lack of resources to sustain a population of large animals can allow smaller members of a species to survive. These circumstances are common on islands, making insular dwarfism the most common form of phyletic dwarfism. (The inverse process, wherein small animals become larger, is called insular gigantism. An excellent example of this is the dodo, the ancestors of which were normal-sized pigeons, but which adapted to life in Madagascar, with its lack of predators, by growing larger and becoming flightless. The dodo quickly became extinct when humans arrived in Madagascar, bringing with them dogs who easily picked off the slow-moving, ground-dwelling birds and rats, which feasted on their eggs.)

In the case of sauropods, the shifting of the Earth's plates, creating smaller landmasses, led to their evolution. The greatest examples of phyletic dwarfism surround us every day: the birds we see are all descendents of the giant dinosaurs we see in museums. Over the last 60 million years, sauropods have dramatically reduced in size but during the last 10 million years some grew again; now on average these saurs are half the size they were in the time of the dinosaurs.

Diplodocs

Diplodocs are long-necked, whip-tailed sauropods, similar in appearance to brachiosaurs. Like brachios, diplodocs are enormous in size, but they can be distinguished from

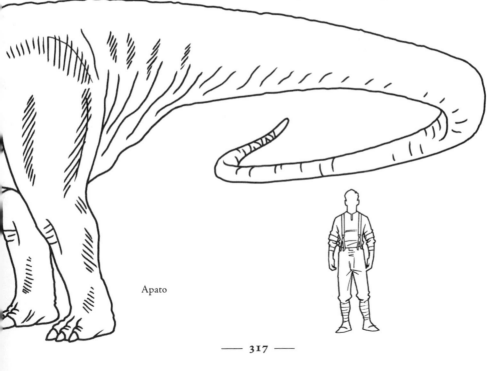

Apato

the former by their 'double-beamed' structure: their long necks and tails are in proportion, giving the appearance of balance. Their front legs are only a little smaller than their back legs, giving their backs a very slight downward slope, unlike the brachios' more pronounced angles. Diplodocs have claws on the first three toes on each foot.

The most prominent members of the diplodoc family are the Apato, Bronto, Baro, Haplo, Diplo and the Supro, which is the largest of all, and perhaps better known as the Supersaur. These members of the family differ in their overall sizes, the shapes of their heads, hollowness of their brows (creating different calls) and the formation of their teeth (specialised for eating different fauna).

Their extremely long necks allow them to reach into dense stands of trees and graze over a broad arc, rather than reaching up into the canopy as a brachios would. Their heads, like those of other sauropods, are relatively tiny compared to the size of their bodies, with the nasal openings on the top of the snout. Their teeth are only present in the front of the mouth, and range in formation between pencil- or peg- shapes, depending on the prominent food supply.

Diplodocs long, whip-like tails are thick at the base and taper off thinly, capable of producing a cracking sound of over 200 decibels, comparable to the volume of a cannon being fired. This sound is used as both part of a mating ritual and to warn off predators. Older diplodocs often have fused or damaged tail vertebrae as a result of a lifetime of cracking their tails.

THERIZINO
Omnivore | Biped

Therizinos are bird-like bipeds, closely related to oviraptors, but with distinctive characteristics that give them an unusual appearance. Therizinos have small beaked heads on long thin necks, yet relatively heavy-set bodies and large, claw-bearing forelimbs. Other notable aspects of the physiology of these saurs include a bird-like pelvis, robust hindlimbs with four toes on each foot, and a stocky tail. Their thick, dense feathers are suitable for cold climates and they use their forelimbs and powerful claws for digging out hibernating ground-dwelling insects and tubular plant roots. Fossils have been found throughout China, Mongolia and the United States, and show that this unique family of saurs were once carnivores and as large as tyrants. Now all common therizinos (usually referred to as zinos) are considerably smaller, no more than the size of a large dog, and found throughout the northern hemisphere. The only exception is the Great Zino, once believed extinct and truly the last of the giants.

Great Zino

Standing at an average of 4 metres tall, and with claws over 80cm in length, the Great Zino is the largest of the therizinos. Some mature males have been known to grow over 5.5 metres tall, with claws of over 1 metre long, perfectly adapted to rip apart the hardest of termite mounds, tear apart fallen trees to uncover grubs and dig out deep pits to nest in. Males and females form bonded pairs who mate for life. Both parents take it in turns to incubate clutches of eggs in deep nesting holes, while the other feeds and cares for the young. In the wild, from a clutch of fifteen eggs, on average only three Great Zino chicks reach a year in age, and only one survives to its second year. Smaller species of common zino have more luck raising their young, perhaps thanks to being more adept at finding smaller insects and plants as food sources.

In recent years the Great Zino has made a remarkable comeback. In captivity a Great Zino can rear its chicks more successfully, with an average of ten reaching two years of age or older. Today, Great Zinos have been re-introduced to Greenland, most Nordic countries, China, Russia and North America. This remarkable conservation success story was begun by a small group of Native Americans in North America, who dedicated themselves to protecting breeding pairs, allowing them to live undisturbed. When their mission came to light in the late 1930s, it became the birth of a movement in North America to preserve the habitat of many of the remaining large wild saurs, and also to promote better understanding and care standards for domesticated saurs. The 'Save the Saurs' movement grew around the world; today it is the largest charitable group dedicated to the protection of saurs in existence.

Great Zino

TRITOP
Herbivore | Quadruped

Tritops are sturdy quadrupeds from the ceratop group, with a thick tail and short, strong limbs: they have three hooves on each forefoot, and four hooves on each hind foot. What makes them unmistakable are the elaborate horns and bony frills covering their necks, used for display, defence and heat regulation. The orientation, configuration, colour and size of their horns and frill show remarkable variation between the sub-species. Most tritops have either long, triangular frills and well-developed brow horns, or conversely shorter and more rectangular frills with elaborate spines and well-developed nasal horns.

Tritops live in large grazing herds and have complicated social structures and ranked hierarchies. Due to their succulent meat and versatile hides, it is believed that these were the first saurs to be domesticated for use as livestock by early humans, and some of the oldest neolithic cave paintings depict tritops in hunting scenes. Selective breeding across generations has created triptop hybrids better suited for meat and leather production, as well as for use in a variety of sports and as agricultural labour.

Western (Californian) Longhorn

The Western (or Californian) Longhorn is a variety of tritop known for its excellent meat and quality hides. It has long brow horns, a triangular nose horn, a prominent epoccipital fringe (ridge of bones surrounding its frill) and pale white soft skin with a purple hue due to its dark, reddish-blue flesh.

The Californian Longhorn is by far the most successful hybrid of all the Western Tritops, and in 2009, the Californian Longhorn became one of the first livestock saur to have a fully mapped genome. When European settlers landed in North America they introduced versatile 'three-horned' ceratops to the continent. The Dutch introduced the popular Western Shorthorn, and the English the hardy Highland Longhorn. The French brought with them the Burgundy Tritops, named for both its birthplace of origin and its colour, and the Spanish introduced the muscular Taurotops. All four varieties produce excellent eggs, meat and hides and are well suited to the American climate. These four varieties of tritops have been interbred over the years and now many varieties of regional tritops dominate the continent, using place names to describe them similar to the regional pure breeds that still exist in France.

The meat produced from the California Longhorn became a household name around the world, thanks to modern mass farming methods, and clever branding and advertising. Between 1935 and

California
Longhorn Tritop

1955 the State of California mass-produced vast quantities of fertilized eggs so farmers outside the region could rear these saurs for profit. During the Second World War, the popularity of the meat exploded as farmers outside California cashed in on its cheap availability. However, since 1964, a Californian Longhorn can only be officially recognized if the saur has been raised within the State of California. This change in legislation ended the export of fertilized eggs and many ranches outside of California have had to change the names of their herds to survive.

The most commonly adopted name throughout the world today is the Western Longhorn, or American Longhorn. Today, although the 'official' Californian Longhorn has fallen from favour, reintroduction of pure breeds of tritops and stytops has helped halt declining numbers. According to an estimate from 2011, there are 1.1 billion tritops in the world, and together the Californian Longhorn and the American or Western Longhorn make up a third of this total.

TYRANT (AMERICAN)
Carnivore | Biped

Tyrants have short, muscular S-shaped necks to support their massive heads, and powerful jaws able to exert the largest bite-force of any terrestrial animal. Their wide barrel chest is supported by powerful hind legs with three weight-bearing toes (among the longest in proportion to body size of any saur) and balanced by a long, heavy tail. They have powerful but short forelimbs with two clawed fingers. To compensate for its immense bulk, many bones throughout the tyrant's skeleton are hollow, reducing weight without significant loss of strength.

Mountain Lythronax (or Golden or Mountain Tyrant)

The American Mountain Lythronax dominates the higher and more inhospitable mountainous regions of North America. With the longest and strongest forelimbs of any tyrant, Mountain Tyrants (or Golden Tyrants, as they are popularly known), use their evolutionary advantage to cling to, balance on and scale rock faces that other tyrants cannot traverse. Their bodies are covered in short, tightly interlocked golden feathers, which give them a smooth appearance similar to a mountain lion (also known as a puma or cougar), with whom they share their habitat. By way of contrast, the Andes Mountain Lythronax of South America are almost white, and have slightly less muscular forearms. Jutting from the back of their lower legs and forelimbs are longer, sturdy feathers primarily used to groom their fur-like feather coat. In common with all ronax tyrants,

Mountain Lythronax

the Mountain Lythronax has a wide head with a short, narrow snout, allowing its eyes to perceive depth through overlapping vision. Other tyrants, such as the White Titan or Dwarf Black, must tilt their heads from side to side to see; ronax tyrants are unique in their ability to see clearly without being hampered by physical limitation.

The Mountain Lythronax lives and hunts in single-sex packs. Female packs and male packs often come into conflict where hunting territories overlap. During the short spring breeding season, a temporary truce allows just enough time for procreation. Males have thicker feathers around their necks; the female has a paler belly. A strict dominance hierarchy keeps the pack in order and increases its chances of successfully chasing prey up into the mountains. Often the alpha male or female may concede its greater portion to the pack in order to gain favour when food is scarce, negating any need for younger rivals to compete for dominance. At its most extreme, in times of acute hardship, an emancipated alpha has been known to lie down to be consumed by its ravenous pack. This gesture could be perhaps read as selflessness, or perhaps pragmatism, knowing that any challenge to its leadership would ultimately be met with its demise. Either way, it is an extraordinary phenomenon and only observed relatively recently.

Brown (Plains) Tyrant

The Brown Tyrant, or Plains Tyrant as it is sometimes known, once was a common sight in large, open territories. Now there are only two surviving species left in the world: the American Brown Tyrant and the Russian Brown Tyrant. Hunted close to extinction during the nineteenth and twentieth centuries, numbers of Brown Tyrants have since rebounded; the Russian Brown owing its survival, in part, to the Chernobyl Exclusion Zone surrounding the nuclear power plant, where radioactive contamination is highest and public access and inhabitation are restricted. This has become a wildlife preserve for tyrants and other rare animals, though poaching has become a threat in recent years. American Brown Tyrants, known locally as the 'Plain Brown' (in this usage, 'plain' is a substitute for 'common' rather than a reference to the Great Plains the tyrants once roamed in huge numbers) are solitary, an adaption to their behaviour that suits their low numbers. In the past, these saurs lived in such large social groups that it was reported in 1836 that a herd migrating near Oakbridge in Ohio was so vast it took ten days to pass the town.

The Brown Tyrant has heavy, dry body feathers that naturally clump together to form thick coats during the bitterly cold winter season. By spring, the coats have become so heavy the Brown Tyrant

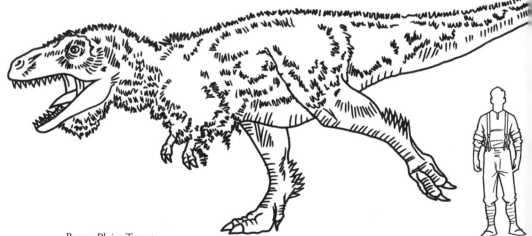

Brown Plains Tyrant

can appear almost double its natural weight and stature. With the onset of summer, and the increase in temperature, Brown Tyrants shed their winter coats, as they sweat more natural oils, loosening their feathers, which fall out in clumps. The Russian Brown retains its winter coat for longer than its American counterpart, as the warmer season begins earlier in North America. Under the tyrant's brown feathers is a soft purple skin, which differs between the sexes; the female has a paler shade, and males tend to have dark tonal patches.

The Brown Tyrant is no longer listed as endangered, but this does not mean the species is secure. The American Brown currently numbers only 800, separated into remote reserves managed with active conservation measures. Brown Tyrants hunt and consume a large amount of prey, and not only are they considered a trophy kill themselves, they are in competition with the same hunters for large wildlife such as bears and deer. Keeping balance in these populations is proving to be a difficult task. Local government controls the numbers by issuing limited permits for the chance to kill Brown Tyrants, but in some areas there have been rumours of deliberate 'technical errors' that have allowed large numbers of permits to kill tyrants to be offered to trophy hunters willing to pay for the privilege.

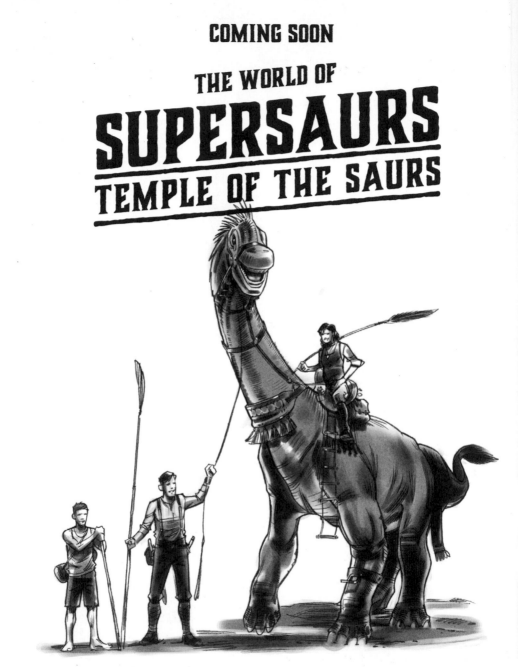

COMING SOON

THE WORLD OF
SUPERSAURS
TEMPLE OF THE SAURS

A lost city in the Mexico jungle reveals surprising secrets . . .